Scent of a Woman

Giovanni Arpino (1927–87) was a novelist, journalist and poet. He won Italy's prestigious Strega Prize in 1964 for *L'ombra della colline* (*The Shadow of Hills*). *Scent of a Woman* (1969), his most famous book, was filmed in 1979 by Diho Risi, starring Vittorio Gassman, and remade in 1992 by Martin Brest, starring Al Pacino.

Anne Milano Appel, a translator and former library director, translates from Italian to English.

GIOVANNI ARPINO

Scent of a Woman

Translated by Anne Milano Appel

PENGUIN BOOKS

PENGUIN CLASSICS

Published by the Penguin Group
Penguin Books Ltd, 80 Strand, London WC2R ORL, England
Penguin Group (USA) Inc., 375 Hudson Street, New York, New York 10014, USA
Penguin Group (Canada), 90 Eglinton Avenue East, Suite 700, Toronto, Ontario, Canada M4P 2Y3
(a division of Pearson Penguin Canada Inc.)
Penguin Ireland, 25 St Stephen's Green, Dublin 2, Ireland (a division of Penguin Books Ltd)
Penguin Group (Australia), 250 Camberwell Road, Camberwell, Victoria 3124, Australia
(a division of Pearson Australia Group Pty Ltd)
Penguin Books India Pvt Ltd, 11 Community Centre, Panchsheel Park,
New Delhi – 110 017, India
Penguin Group (NZ), 67 Apollo Drive, Rosedale, Auckland 0632, New Zealand
(a division of Pearson New Zealand Ltd)
Penguin Books (South Africa) (Pty) Ltd, 24 Sturdee Avenue, Rosebank, Johannesburg 2196,
South Africa

Penguin Books Ltd, Registered Offices: 80 Strand, London WC2R ORL, England

www.penguin.com

First published as *Il buio e il miele* in Italy 1969
This translation first published in Penguin Classics 2011

Set in 12/14.75 pt Dante MT
Typeset by Ellipsis Books Limited, Glasgow
Printed in England by Clays Ltd, St Ives plc

ISBN: 978-0-141-19318-2

www.greenpenguin.co.uk

'. . . it is our task to impress this provisional, transient earth upon ourselves so deeply, so agonizingly, and so passionately that its essence rises up again "invisibly" within us. We are the bees of the invisible. We ceaselessly gather the honey of the visible to store it in the great golden hive of the Invisible.'

Rilke, from a letter of 1925

'It may be that any other salvation than that which comes from where the danger is, is still within the unholy.'

Heidegger, *What are poets for?*

I

A large iridescent fly buzzed around the window on the landing; the walls smelled of fresh paint. Relishing the taste of air, the fly veered suddenly, found the narrow gap at the partially open window, and disappeared. I leaned out too, to toss away my cigarette butt. The courtyard below was deserted: a meagre couple of yards of cement in the late August sun. In the distance, the withered green of the hills beyond the river blended into an opaque sky. Before ringing the doorbell, I felt to make sure my cap was sitting firmly on my forehead, checked the knot and proper positioning of my tie.

The door opened at once, as if the woman had been there all along, waiting.

She was a tiny old woman, incredibly rosy and diminutive, dressed in white and grey. Smiling and twinkling through every one of her delightful wrinkles, she gestured for me to come in. Behind her, the darkness of a long corridor. We quickly turned into a kitchen, two chairs already moved out from the table.

'Good, good, very punctual, that's a pleasure to see.' She sighed, still smiling, nodding, her hands clasped.

I told her my name and carefully balanced my cap on my knee.

'But you're hardly more than a boy, good heavens!' she lamented, squinting. I felt myself blush. 'Who knows whether a young man like you will have the patience that this situation . . . the patience to stay here.'

She remained undecided, holding her breath, her lips slightly parted over her porcelain teeth.

So I told her that my commanding officer at the barracks had explained the situation to me in detail.

Her smile faded, she nodded again, stroking the back of her right hand with the slender fingers of her left. She had very beautiful hands, transparent as tissue-paper, in keeping with her, with the immaculate surroundings, with the two flowers in the vase on the table.

'A student, I think. An only child?'

I told her a little about my father, a clerk, about my mother and my younger sister. As I searched for the right words, those three familiar faces emerged from their usual misty haze for a moment, only to become softly shrouded again soon afterwards. I then specified my age, twenty years old, and the university faculty I was enrolled in, business and economy.

The voice coming out of my mouth felt unconnected to me.

Her sigh in response was not one of relief.

'I know nothing about today's young people,' she said finally, hedging. 'Him too, him in there, with that great misfortune of his, I can't understand him either. It must be my age. And then too: can understanding help in any way? Sympathy does, of course.'

But as if stung by delirium, she was once again on her feet and smiling, expressions flitting across her face: 'There's chilled coffee, would you like some? It's good. Or maybe an orangeade would be better? Don't tell me you wouldn't like some.'

She was spinning around. I thought: a squirrel. I soon had a glass of coffee in my hands.

'Is it all right if I smoke?'

She laughed quietly. 'Go ahead. Him too, one cigarette after another. You men.'

She accompanied that 'him' with a brief wag of her fingers over her shoulders, as if to indicate the entities hidden beyond the darkness of the corridor.

She recovered her composure, her hands clasped, and continued: 'Still, all in all you give the impression of being a fine young man, fine indeed.'

We went on looking at each other; I was determined not to be the first to ask a question.

Finally she made up her mind to speak, lowering her voice: 'I'm his aunt. He says I'm only a cousin, but in fact I'm like an aunt and more, because who nursed his poor mother up until the end, if not me? Fortunately she passed away before having to endure the worst. Afterwards it was all so difficult, no one can ever imagine. Until the day of the accident I didn't know him very well. He was always roaming around the world, boarding school, academy, the military. But since then I've had to be the one to look after him, it's clear that God above willed it. It's been nine years now, did you know that?'

I finished the coffee, and went on holding the glass in my hand. It was still cool.

'Nine years,' she went on in a monotone, her voice increasingly thinner. 'Today it's nothing, but at the beginning: oh, I don't even want to think about how it was at the beginning. A young man like him, losing his sight and a hand. Just like that: only because Our Lord won't let anyone be happy in this world. During manoeuvres, playing with a bomb. I say "playing" because what else are these manoeuvres nowadays? Here, give me that glass.'

'My commander explained it to me,' I said.

In order to appear indifferent, I stared at the tiles on the floor. Each set of four formed a blue design, a kind of improvised flower against a white background. Through the transparent curtains at the window the light fell on those flowers in a sunburst, revealing their fragility.

'A man like him,' she went on slowly, as the wrinkles on her face crumpled and unfolded. 'Even rather wealthy, yes. He's rich, I'm certainly not. A scrap of widow's pension, that's all I have. But him: rich. Not even forty years old. Healthy as a horse. And all alone in the world.'

Carefully I crushed out the butt in the little plate she had offered me as an ashtray.

'Take good care of him during this time, please,' she added. 'You must never leave him alone. You know that, don't you? And be patient, young man, very, very patient. Don't contradict him, don't argue for heaven's sake! Always tell him he's right, whether he's making sense or raving. The only sure way out is to always answer yes. Yes and yes, sir. Do you understand?'

'Of course, ma'am.'

'Ciccio, the soldier who is in hospital right now, his attendant up until the day before yesterday, was Calabrian, thick-headed but good, in some cases even cunning. He realized right away that his only reply must be "yes" and "yes, sir". That Ciccio too, though: coming down with typhus just now, on the eve of the trip. Does that sound like luck to you?'

'In our barracks too there have been three cases of typhus,' I said, immediately noticing her lack of interest.

Her watery eyes were fixed on me, as though seeking some image beyond me.

In a wispy voice, she offered: 'Bad is a strong word, and I wouldn't want to actually say he's bad, but he's cut from different cloth, nothing in common with people like us. The great damage he's suffered, of course. But he was a little like that even before the accident: God knows what his mother had to put up with, raising him. Then too, the pain. But these are our secrets, right, my boy?'

'Thank you, ma'am.'

She continued gazing at me with fleeting tenderness, then sudden mistrust. She set down the glass, and carefully and repeatedly smoothed the cuffs of her dress, her fingers lightly ironing out invisible creases.

Maybe she was afraid she'd said too much.

In fact: 'For you, after all, it's also a nice vacation,' she added, looking away. 'Five days plus two, as you say – in short, a week's leave is something, to be sure. All the way to Naples, and no barracks.'

She was right, so I tried to utter another reassuring phrase.

'Fine, fine,' she interrupted, suddenly dejected, 'now you'd better go in. There are strips of cloth right outside there. For polishing. With those heavy military boots of yours. It's the door at the end of the corridor. But knock first. Always knock first, with him. I . . . it's best if I stay here. God help me, something always slips out of this mouth of mine.'

She had already shut me out of her orbit. With an elbow

planted on the table, she was now admiring the two flowers in the vase, the fingertips of her right hand reaching out to touch and examine petal after petal.

'And never call him captain, always just sir,' she warned again blankly, not looking at me.

'I'll call you Ciccio. Do you like that? I've always called all of you that. Or do you mind? Does it seem like a dog's name? If you don't like it, say so. Go ahead and tell me.'

He'd had me sit down and his pitted face was less than a few feet away. The dark glasses that wrapped around his temples and his gloved, rigid left hand gleamed faintly in the semi-darkness. His smile flashed readily, quickly erasing the effect of a face that only appeared smooth – and very pale – between the hairline and the top of his glasses.

From the window, beyond the curtain, faint street noises could be heard.

'Warm? Did you have something to drink in there? Say something. Are you or aren't you a student? So then, talk.'

He ended with a laugh.

'Yes, sir,' I said.

His right hand reached towards the table that stood between us and he took a cigarette from the pack. Before I could strike a match, those fingers swiftly moved to measure the distance between his lips and the tip of the cigarette, flicked on a lighter, flipped it shut, and like elegant elytrons fell back and closed around the gloved hand in his lap.

'Do you walk? Do you know how to walk? I had a certain Ciccio last year who absolutely couldn't at all. Hopeless. After an hour he was already puffing. I on the other hand have a great need to walk. I could wear out a horse. You all think

you know how to move but when put to the test: it's torture.'
He laughed again, blowing smoke.

'I walk, yes. At the barracks . . .'

'None of that barracks shit—' he interrupted, raising a
hand. 'Or maybe so? Tell me, tell me.'

'It wasn't anything important.' I retreated.

He doubled over in a burst of laughter until a coughing
fit forced him to sit back up on the sofa. He wiped the corners
of his mouth with a handkerchief.

'Magnificent!' he said then, showing his teeth. 'We have a
Ciccio who thinks. A prudent Ciccio. Of course, a student.
I had another one, some time ago. Philosophy: a real pain in
the neck. You don't seem like a pain in the neck. I'll bet you
think you're shrewd.'

'Not always, sir,' I thought I should answer.

'Capricorn?'

'No, Aquarius,' I said.

His lips curled in a grimace.

'You too, an Aquarian. This won't work. Two Aquarians
together make nasty sparks fly. I don't want to know which
decade. Not for any reason in the world. Your lips are sealed,
never let your decade slip out.'

'Fine,' I replied.

He coughed weakly. 'Aquarian. From Piedmont. Business
and Economy no less. And since you're here, a humanitarian
on top of it. I don't get you, Ciccio. But why should I have
to understand you? We're under no obligation to understand
each other, right? For a week, five days plus two: all we have
to do is be able to tolerate one another. And walk at a trot.
Right?'

'Right.'

'No, not right,' he shot back triumphantly. 'You'll see why. Nevertheless, tomorrow, at seven. Here. Then the station, then Genoa, Rome, Naples. Been there?'

'Not to Naples.'

'Well, now. Finally we'll accompany this Business and Economy Aquarian to someplace new. I was beginning to give up hope.' He smiled, the cigarette clamped between his teeth.

Every so often his voice cracked into more strident syllables and accents.

'I didn't know we would be stopping in Genoa and Rome. If I understood right,' I went on.

'Stopping? Who said we were stopping? If I feel like it. If I get the urge. To walk and have a good time. Five days plus two: what do you care how you spend them? Were you hoping to shave a little something off the total? Are there some little sluts waiting for you? Tell me, tell me.'

'No. No one waiting. I was just saying.'

'Ciccio was just saying.' He began getting to his feet with a broad yawn.

He was extremely thin, a twisted wire inside a jacket and trousers which accentuated his thinness even more. His tendons burst out of his shirt collar like props supporting his head.

Calmly he crossed the room, opened a cabinet and a bottle, poured a large glass of whisky and emptied half of it immediately. He sighed deeply before downing it completely. From the surrounding shadows an enormous grey cat appeared, approaching him soundlessly. It stopped in front of him, its tail swishing slowly back and forth on the floor.

'This is the Baron,' he explained, setting the glass back

down. 'Some monument, huh? Six years old. A colossus. Castrated. He hates my guts but watch out if I'm not here, if he doesn't hear my voice. And when I am here, he always tries to trip me. He's never managed to, poor Baron.'

The animal studied him, its face turned up, an electric charge running through its tail.

'Angry as usual, huh?' he said, bending over stiffly. He petted the cat, scratching the back of its neck between the ears. 'Ugly eunuch. Vicious rascal. Tomorrow I'm leaving. You'll see, the nice lady will put you on a diet. No more chopped meat. Fat roly-poly.'

The cat quivered, fuming. In distress it escaped the hand and disappeared into a corner.

'He understands everything. I insult him and he hates me. Or vice versa.' He laughed. From somewhere a rather short, flexible bamboo cane had already appeared in his hand.

He smiled, suddenly sad, tapping his calf with the tip of the cane. 'I won't deny that I would have preferred a level-headed country boy from the mountains. But maybe you'll be an exception. We'll see. Stand up.'

Before I could step forward he held out the bamboo cane, stopping me. He brushed my shoulder lightly with the tip.

'You're small. What the hell. Little more than a dwarf. Some Aquarian you are, a fake. How can we manage to walk with two different compasses?' He swore.

Twisting his mouth he ran over me again with the bamboo cane, from shoulder to knee. His gloved hand was supported between the top two buttons of his jacket.

'Bah. Let's give it a try.'

He opened the door to the corridor, immediately kicking and swearing as he sent the strips of cloth behind it flying. I moved closer and with a swift, sure move his gloved hand slid under my right arm. I felt the rigidity of those bones, the tense nerves, the stiff bulge of iron and leather that bound the prosthesis just above his wrist. The sudden tug nearly made me lose my balance.

'Idiot. What are you made of? Sawdust?' he said, stopping. 'Where do you think you're going? To a procession? Walking is walking. Look sharp!'

We dashed ahead through the corridor, steps in sync, our pace faster and faster, with my right shoulder planted against his arm, and the cane held out crosswise to gauge my knee. Every few feet I felt the bamboo tip waiting to check my moving leg. After three laps back and forth he stopped abruptly.

'It's not working. No way,' he decreed, without removing his arm from mine. 'You're not walking. All you're doing is dragging your 130 pounds. If you don't move your legs with some energy, they're almost rigid, get it? You lose your behind, you leave it half a yard away, and you end up worn out after not even half an hour. You're not at a funeral. Come on. Push with your gluteus, for God's sake. Do you know what the gluteus is? Are you afraid to use it?'

We started all over again, and now his cane twirled at regular intervals from my knee to my rear end, checking them in rapid, rhythmic semicircles. At the fifth lap I saw a strip of light appear along the kitchen door and realized that the old woman was watching us intently.

'Once more. And plant your heels on the ground. What are you afraid of? The waxed floor? Plant your heels. Leave their imprint on the wax.'

He stopped suddenly, making me lurch.

'Another thing,' he said, stock-still, the cane raised. 'No wandering in your head. We're walking. There's no need to think. You think sitting down. You have to start and stop exactly in step with me. Understood? Like clockwork. And no sashaying like a streetwalker out for a stroll.'

'Yes, sir,' I said, somehow managing to swallow a comment about the corridor being too dark.

We were back in his room, or maybe his study, where various massive components of a stereo system peered out from the corners. The cat was breathing loudly from beneath the couch. At the cabinet, he poured two glasses of whisky to the brim, and immediately held one out, his right hand extended in space.

'Drink up.'

'Actually I rarely drink. Almost never,' I replied, taking the glass.

'Really? I couldn't care less. Five days plus two: with me you'll drink. And no objections. When you can't take any more, dump it out somewhere. In your pocket maybe. As long as I don't notice.' He laughed soundlessly.

I barely took a sip, then twisting my arm with the utmost caution, tried to set the glass on the table.

'Hang on, Ciccio. Are you trying to be smart?' He smiled calmly from the centre of the room. 'Not with me, boy. Never with me. Finish it, now. And hand it back empty. A twelve-year-old whisky, you must be kidding.'

I drank some more, on my feet as well, a few steps away from him. I tried not to look at him, taking advantage of the darkness that made him seem transparent. His face had faded away towards the top, a grey film with no geometry.

'Does it burn?'

'No, sir,' I replied.

'You're skinny. A skeleton. Bones are too sharp. I'll get bruised up walking with you. I'll fatten you up with whisky. However, I must admit that you don't stink. The other Ciccio, your predecessor with typhus: ghastly. Every day before we went out I had to pour half a quart of cologne down his back. He smelled like a pigsty, like reheated minestrone.'

Ten minutes later I was out in the street, my eyes heavy, unable to orient myself. I had time before having to return to the base. I cursed the nothingness outside and inside me.

Standing on the sidewalk, before taking a step in the moist, sticky air, I looked for a friendly sign, a café.

2

'If only it would rain. Damn it. A million bucks for a deluge,' he kept muttering.

We were sitting opposite each other on the shaded side of the compartment. The wind drove scorching breaths through the lowered windows. Another hour to go, then Genoa. The flat countryside, at times swelling abruptly with bristling hills, whirled by in the morning light as though under an ashen umbrella.

He had been complaining and disparaging from the beginning: the vile, odious summer, the scratchy velvet seats, the deserted coach. The high speed of the express train, which shook the cars, prevented any attempt at walking in the corridor.

He sat motionless, smoking one cigarette after another, his gloved hand on the armrest, a faint layer of perspiration on his forehead. In the bright light the marks on his face no longer seemed like real scars but like blotches and traces of smallpox. And yet, during certain imperceptible movements, that head appeared more than handsome: a prism that picked up and fashioned not so much the external luminosity as the leaps and moods, the odd angles of his thoughts.

He held out his right hand.

'Do you have a wallet? Let me feel it.'

I took it out, surprised, and placed it in contact with his fingers. He slid it into the palm of his hand.

'How much money?'

I told him the amount.

With a single gesture he opened it, took out the few bills and handed them to me.

'Here. Are your ID cards and driver's licence in here?' he continued brusquely.

'Yes, sir.'

'I'll hold on to it.' He smiled, satisfied, relaxing and slipping the wallet into his pocket. 'You can depend on me more. Right? I'll give you a new one, at the end. Don't worry. If you're angry now, say so.'

'No, sir,' I replied.

'Don't give me that cock and bull.' He chuckled softly. 'I know very well you're angry. Anyone would be. You might as well admit it.'

'Okay. If it matters to you. I am.'

He laughed more heartily.

'Finally,' he coughed. 'But you have to admit that I also have to try and protect myself. You could get fed up, leave me high and dry in the middle of a street, a café, maybe here in the train. I don't know you, after all.'

'I'm not that type,' I protested.

'Maybe not. Who knows. And then you'd be punished. A nice stint in solitary confinement, as you know,' he said, the cigarette wobbling between his lips. 'So at least allow me the illusion of being able to protect myself. If you look at it that way: is it okay with you?'

'Whatever you say, sir.'

'It's not at all okay with you, yet your "yessir" flows out easily just the same. You're made of rubber, Ciccio. You take it and snap! you spring back the way you were. I bet your father was a peasant. Right?'

'He's a clerk,' I said.

'Then your grandfather was.'

'He had a shop, my grandfather.'

'Well, your great-grandfather then. Let's not go on and on,' he said irritably. 'You're too cautious. Too many peasant-like "yes, sirs", I can tell. Peasants in fact always say yes, and while they're digging for potatoes they're also digging their grave. Forever complaining about it, of course.'

I kept quiet, and for a long moment busied myself choosing, fingering and lighting a cigarette.

'You're not speaking any more? Good boy,' he went on. 'Tell the truth: if there had been someone else in this idiotic compartment, would you have said "yessir" and "nossir" like you did before, about the wallet? Or not?'

'Why not? Other people mean nothing to me,' I replied.

He indulged in a broad, tolerant laugh, nodding spiritedly.

'You're opening up. Good for you.' He coughed again. 'So then, tell me, tell me: you've decided that it's better to feel sorry, and so on, for this poor devil here. Right?'

'No, sir.'

'Look, look at me: don't you pity me?' He smiled, pouting ironically.

'I don't know, sir. I don't think so.'

'You see, I told you you're made of rubber,' he retorted, satisfied. 'C'mon: you don't feel sorry for me, sorry in the sense of pitying me, I mean, and besides that, you obey, you do your duty, you're ready with a "yessir", et cetera, et cetera, therefore you feel you're doing the right thing. Is that it?'

'What I meant was: you don't make me feel sorry or pity you in some stupid way,' I tried to explain.

'Of course. Naturally. Let's see then. Earlier I said: a million bucks for a deluge. What did you think I meant?' He leaned forward a little, smiling curiously.

'I thought you meant what you said. Something to relieve this heat,' I replied.

'Not at all, genius. Aside from the fact that a deluge, *the* deluge, would always be good. Aside from that I meant the light, not the heat. The heat is only a result. It's the light I was talking about,' he explained, stressing each syllable, 'light is silent, horribly silent. Whereas rain produces sounds. With rain, you always know where you are. Shut up at home or huddling in some doorway. Do you get it? Now don't you feel sorry for me?'

'Yes, sir. For that, yes,' I forced myself to respond.

My head was spinning from those rapid-fire words of his. I could still hear them buzzing.

He had relaxed against the padded seat back, suddenly bored.

'Right. Drop dead,' he then said slowly. 'I meant me, not you. Why do I bother talking. I should cut out my tongue.'

Again he cheered up in that wicked way of his, stuck his tongue out a little and with his right hand forming a scissor, made as if to snip it off, laughing the whole time.

He stopped and made a face.

Then: 'Your hair, is it black?'

'Not actually black. Brown.'

'See how black mine is? A raven,' he said proudly. 'And women like black hair. It's virile, they say.'

Suddenly he bent his forehead down.

'Hey. No white hairs by any chance?'

'Not even one, sir.'

I felt nauseous from the cigarettes I'd smoked and a little hungry too. I thought about the sandwich in my duffel bag, but I didn't dare stand up, take it out and eat it there in front of him. He on the other hand took a slim metal and leather flask out of his breast pocket, unscrewed the cap, and drank.

'Horrible at this hour.' He shuddered. 'If you see one of those railway bozos pass by, call him.'

He leaned his temple to one side to rest, but instead a range of expressions flitted across his face.

We passed through a succession of tunnels. The compartment was swept with currents of damp air. A large oily drop left a mark on my pants, another one grazed his forehead.

'We'll get off at Genoa. You can go nuts in here,' he grumbled, still leaning sideways. 'And you will also do me a blessed favour and take off your uniform. I mean, you must have civilian clothes.'

'No, sir.'

'I'll buy you some.' He snorted. 'I don't want to appear to be in the care of the nation's charitable hands.'

He took out his watch, opened it and fingered it.

The sea reappeared on the right, a thin layer of metallic grey beyond a jumbled group of houses.

'A conductor,' I told him.

He raised his hand to stop him.

The man stepped forward with a long, sad face. A gold stripe ran around his cap. He gave a sympathetic smile.

'Mr Whatever-your-name-is,' he assailed him in a quiet cutting voice, 'is it obligatory to listen to this crap? Have they passed a law requiring it?'

'Pardon me, sir?' The man blinked.

'I repeat: this crap. This public nuisance.' With his gloved hand he gave a sharp blow to the padded seat near his temple.

'The radio, sir?' The man figured it out.

'Loathsome. Turn it off right now,' came the reply.

'Of course. But you see, you have to turn them all off. The controls are in the dining car and at this hour . . .' the man stammered.

'Do you want me to shoot a pistol in it?' He stretched out his neck, his voice a strangled hiss. 'What does turn it off mean? It means *off*. So hurry it up.'

'Certainly, sir, but at this hour . . .' The man was dismayed. He tried in vain to meet my eyes to find some support.

I felt myself blush. I remained rigid against the seat back.

'I lost my eyes and a hand for the honour of this rotten country. Did I or didn't I? Now you want me to lose my hearing too?' he shouted suddenly.

He had become livid, two saliva bubbles at the corners of his mouth.

'Right away, sir, right away.' The conductor fled, his fingers touching his cap in an awkward salute.

Then he relaxed with pleasure, his right hand carefully assuring that the left one lined up precisely with the armrest. He was laughing quietly, in abrupt, self-satisfied little fits that finally erupted into short bursts of coughing.

'Bastard that I am. The greatest one-of-a-kind bastard,' he said, enjoying himself. 'Who knows what he'll tell them at home tonight, that poor devil.'

I leaned my head back myself to absorb the sounds from the velvet that I had not noticed until then. Barely a wisp of music came out, which I could hear only by pressing my ear forcefully against it. Until I heard nothing more.

Almost without being aware of it, I opened my mouth wide, savouring the syllables of the words I mutely swore at him.

'Who knows how nervous the Baron must be.' He cheered up again. 'Without me in that house, they all immediately get addled.'

Taking a long curve, the train slowed up as it came into Genoa. The sun flashed off the junctions of the tracks, and off the sidewalks of the station. Dusty pots of geraniums clustered along a wall.

As I took down the suitcases, I saw him recompose himself, his hand feeling the knot of his necktie, then a handkerchief to wipe his forehead.

He gave me some final orders.

'You're not with me to be a porter. Get one outside: that's what they're there for. We're off to the hotel right opposite the station. The one with the palm tree. One of the few that still has connecting rooms. You'll have to plug your ears to sleep. You can hear a few thousand trains go by.'

3

Shortly after noon the wind picked up, sudden, torrid gusts that tore in, raising dense swirls of dust, paper, dry leaves, and ruffling the foliage of the trees in the middle of the piazza.

'Marvellous!' he said, delighted, taking in the first breath of air. But we soon withdrew inside the café.

Through the windows, beneath a sky that was becoming more lively, I saw a sliver of the harbour, a crane, the stern of a rusty ship. Tiny flags fluttered in a row, straining against the wind's constant lacerations.

We had already been to a shop where, at vast expense, he had bought a pale blue suit and a shirt for me, a white linen suit for himself. They would be delivered to us at the hotel by that evening, after a few adjustments and stitching up the trouser cuffs. We had then walked swiftly down a sloping street, he cheerfully and silently waving the cane in front of him, his arm under mine, increasingly prodding me to step up the pace.

'And this afternoon, a good barber,' he said in a satisfied tone.

By now, the receipts on the table for the various drinks formed a kind of fan anchored by the ashtray. The waiter arrived with a fifth of whisky.

'Are we eating at one?' I asked. My head was spinning from the two vermouths I had drunk shortly before.

'Right. Food. You must be hungry,' he replied, jiggling the ice in his glass. 'Who knows if I was that hungry when I was your age. I can't remember a thing. No recollection. I'll give you an hour's leave. For now I'm not eating. Go to the counter and see if they have any decent sandwiches. But don't have them brought to me: just look.'

I got up. There were sandwiches of various kinds under large plastic lids. Lettuce leaves peeked out from the edges. The young man behind the counter wore a stained, filthy apron. He was examining his hair, faithfully reflected in the bottles behind him. He glanced at me a second with that indifference that everyone displays towards a soldier: a transparent entity who doesn't even disturb the view.

'There are a few. Not very clean,' I said when I returned.

'A little dirt is the least of it in these parts. So then, scram.' He sent me off, handing me some money: 'Here. Eat. Go to the port, so you can take a look at the girls.'

'What girls?' I asked, surprised.

'The usual. Never heard of them?' he mocked, but good-naturedly. 'There are droves of them at every large port. Dark-skinned too if you want. In short, *those* girls.'

'I'd rather eat!' I laughed.

He shrugged, annoyed.

'I meant, while you're walking. Or do you turn the other way when you see them? Born yesterday.'

'All right, sir.'

'Check out a few. You never know,' he concluded drily. He snapped open his watch. 'Be back here at two. No later.'

Outside I bent over against the wind, exhilarated to be

alone and by the thought of the new suit. But as I neared the port, that freedom already seemed unexciting. I realized to my surprise that I would have preferred to see him eat in front of me, I imagined his gestures at the table, the inevitable insolence towards the waiter.

I had the sea to my right, obstructed by port machinery, and a scruffy wall on my left. Keeping close to the wall, I saw several eateries down some narrow steps. I stopped in front of baskets full of shellfish on display; further on a sluggish grey fish floated in two inches of water. A waiter quickly appeared and gave me the once-over, so I started walking again, turning around to glance down the length of the port: colours, prows, rows of smokestacks and cranes, even the wind seemed calculated to me, like a scene in a film. My eyes ached and even the distant din of noises and voices, perhaps from a market beyond the wall, hurt my head which was already pounding from the vermouth. At the next sign I decided to stop. The trattoria was deserted, and from the kitchen doorway the owner gave me an indifferent look.

I felt like I had been gone too long, caught up in a bubble that was not uplifting but oppressive, and I felt vaguely homesick for my city, whether home or the base.

A postcard for my mother, I thought.

I chose quickly from the menu – anything to hurry it up – then sat and waited, looking at the dessert trolley.

'I assure you, sir. Not one grey hair. Allow me . . .' the barber repeated quietly, leaning over. 'Even here at the top, a critical point, everything looks fine.'

'Good, good,' he replied curtly.

The manicurist was already crouching wordlessly at his

right, attending to his nails, filing them, and he, draped in a double sheet, leaned back and let himself be shaved.

I could see his face in the mirror, divided in half by his dark glasses. Little by little the shaving cream hid the scars and those dark pits, tiny, as though made by a gimlet. The barber moved around him with very special care; the girl too worked with concentration.

Until she drew back the nail file in alarm: 'Oh I'm so sorry, sir,' she said, pausing.

'It's nothing, dear. Nothing at all,' he replied gently.

'Did something happen?' the barber asked with concern, gesturing at the girl angrily.

'For heaven's sake, no! Go on, dear. Continue. It's fine,' he said again.

The girl leaned over with a cotton ball, ever more solicitously.

The barber was having a hard time starting a conversation. Two or three times he threw me a look that I was careful not to meet. He was old and pale. In the back of that shop of his, a young errand boy, his hair slick with brilliantine, was reading the sports pages in a secluded corner.

'How was she?' he asked as soon as we left.

He had left a big tip; all three of them had rushed to open the door for us.

'The manicurist? Skinny. Not bad looking, but tiny, not even ninety pounds,' I explained.

'If only I had known. I would have given her a kick. Ugly bitch,' he said through clenched teeth. 'I can't stand the sound of the file to begin with. Imagine when it jabs you.'

We walked briskly though the street was uphill. The wind had died down, the lights opposite the first floors weren't swaying any more. I felt sweaty and a little tired, and I was itching to go back to the hotel and try on the new suit.

Instead he said: 'Feel how fresh the air is. How it should be. Wind – or better yet, rain. Then fresh air like this. That gets you going. Hurray.'

I could depend on his thirst though. The little pocket flask was most certainly no longer full, and in fact we soon sat down at a café. A rectangle of cleansed, luminous sky topped this new unfamiliar piazza; sunset was still a long way off. At one end, near a newspaper stand, a group of tram drivers milled around scoffing at one another in soft lilting voices. The dense maze of trams parked at the end of the line stood in full sunshine, the light splintered through plate-glass windows. It occurred to me: a newspaper, remember to get a newspaper to read in bed tonight. And for some reason the baseness of that thought mortified me.

'I could go for something to eat. But no. Better not. Otherwise I'll have no appetite tonight,' he said, taking a deep breath after his whisky. 'Speaking of which: the girls. Tell me about them.'

'The ones at the port? I didn't see many,' I answered.

I tasted my ice cream, after he made me pour a good inch of liquor over it.

'Snap to, Ciccio.' His voice was calm, but with a restrained seething that was anything but reassuring. 'Your predecessor, illiterate as he was, could find them even under rocks. That's all he could talk about, unfortunately. How could you rely on him? He liked them all. You: loosen your tongue.'

I spoke, trying to remember, and here and there inventing things. I gathered that I would do well to go on talking about a certain woman dressed in orange in the doorway of a bar.

'Was she tall? Very tall?' he asked.

'Tall, yeah. Like you. Very tall.'

'Well go on, for Christ's sake. Are we playing around here? Do I have to drag every word out like pulling teeth?' He lost his patience. Two fingers had already made the glass clink on its plate for a second round. A waiter rushed over.

'I told you everything, I'm sorry. It's not as if I spoke to her,' I said. 'She was at the door of a bar. By herself. Tall. With black hair. Long, thick black hair.'

'Her hair was black. But not her skin. Her skin wasn't too dark, right? Pale skin: the best.' He smiled into space.

'Dark? I don't think so. Pale. Yeah, definitely. Not thin though. All in all, a rather big woman.' I was fed up.

'Just what I wanted to hear!' He laughed excitedly, tapping his foot. 'A fine big woman. But young. That's how I like them, Ciccio. Tomorrow.'

'Tomorrow, what?' I said.

'Tomorrow we'll go look for her. You'll look for her for me. You must remember that bar, for God's sake.' He went on smiling, drumming under the table. 'Wonderful.'

'But I . . .'

'But you, what?'

'I wouldn't know how.'

'Oh, you wouldn't know how. What the hell do you mean? How to talk to her? To that girl?' He laughed, pleased with himself. 'Don't worry. You tell her the truth: no more, no less. She says ten. You come back with fifteen. What are you afraid of? Being taken for a pimp?'

'A pimp? Well, that's not what I meant. I don't know, I guess,' I replied clumsily.

'Don't act like an idiot all of a sudden.' His tone changed, a faint trace of anxiety beneath the usual assurance. His hand moved as if to touch my arm, stopped. 'What harm is there? I don't want to force you. But where's the harm? We go there, you talk to her, then you accompany me there, you wait for me and that's the end of it. Not even an hour, you'll see. Right?'

'Yes, sir.'

He wanted to have dinner before going back to the hotel. At the table, in a melancholy, deserted restaurant, he was soon full after some prosciutto and soup with an egg in it. He toyed with a few grapes without eating any of them. He hardly spoke, distracted, his cigarette smouldering in the ashtray. He had no interest whatever in what I chose, no questions.

His mood changed, however, as we walked back to the hotel. I heard him whistling an old tune, the bamboo cane cheerfully chopping the air in front of us.

The sky had matured into a dark green; in the distance pink and grey walls could be seen sloping in terraces up the hill. But everything I saw seemed unfamiliar to my eyes, images of a world that wasn't mine, even alien to mine, which disappeared soon afterwards without a trace.

He drank some more before going up, and I had to wait beside him at the bar. Hidden behind his newspaper, the guy behind the bar barely glanced at us.

Then: 'Why tomorrow with that girl and not right now?' I threw out. 'Wouldn't now be better? While we're here. Tomorrow we have to leave.'

But he objected in a voice that had become faint and distant.

'No, not tonight. Not at night. Then too, I'm not ready

yet. I have to think about it. We'll leave tomorrow night. But in the afternoon, with our new suits: a nice shot of life. Trust me Ciccio, it will do me good.'

'Yes, sir.'

Upstairs, I walked him all around the room, which he auscultated and mastered in just a few minutes, testing with rapid strokes of his cane. The big bundle of new clothes lay on a chair, impressive in its impeccable wrapping.

'We'll open it and try them on tomorrow. No hurry,' he said tiredly. 'Is the suitcase on the table? That's all for now. Go. I'll call you in half an hour.'

I waited sitting on the bed, not daring to undress. When he called me, he was already in bed, in his pajamas, his gloved left hand on the folded sheet, the ashtray, watch and cigarettes close by.

'You bought a newspaper. From Turin? Good. Sometimes it has the best marriage ads in the world. Sit down. Make yourself comfortable,' he said. 'Read, right now.'

I began: 'Tall bank clerk, F, 39, from the north, athletic, good family, would like to meet a tall . . .' I went on reading until the end of the two half-columns, not stopping despite the fact that my mouth was dry.

He smoked, listening attentively, occasionally letting out a brief laugh, an indecipherable mumble. He nodded, twisting his mouth, waved his hand in the air in ironic approval, false pity. Against the whiteness of the pillowcase, his face stood out as though bruised by the harsh light that flooded the room.

'Cut out the one about the attractive, refined, 4-foot-9, artistic temperament,' he said finally. 'It's definitely one of the good ones. In my suitcase, in the accordion pocket, there's a large envelope. Put it in there. I have hundreds of them. I collect the most amusing ones. When you're feeling down, there's nothing better than having someone reread them all to you.'

I obeyed, and remained standing at the foot of the bed a moment. Through the wall the hum of the elevator found its way in. Voices rose and were swallowed away.

'Go on to bed, Ciccio. Good night,' he said ruefully. 'Oh wait. I was forgetting my good deed.'

He had me bring him the folder containing envelopes and sheets of paper with the hotel's letterhead.

'Do you have a pen?'

He leaned the folder against his knees, holding it firmly with his gloved hand, unfolded a sheet of paper and after carefully feeling its edges with his right index finger, began writing. Slowly, one great big letter after another, none of them connected: an upper-case 'S', then an 'h', an 'i', a 't'...

The slanting stroke of the last letter almost ran off the sheet. 'It's for my aunt. You remember my cousin the aunt,' he said handing me the folder. 'Don't be shocked. She's used to it. She enjoys it. She pretends to get angry and then she complains to the Baron, who becomes hydrophobic. Let's not forget to mail it tomorrow. I'll dictate the address.'

As I wrote, he again broke into a laugh, but coldly.

'Now go. Get some sleep. If you can.' Idly lifting the gloved hand, he added: 'I have to take this off. If only I could remove my head too.'

'If you want I'll help,' I said.

'Don't be ridiculous.' Suddenly he blasted out, teeth clenched: 'Most of all don't be hypocritical. Because that's what you are: a hypocrite. You have no life. You have no blood. A pile of ashes. That's what your twenty years amount to. But I don't give a damn. About you and all those like you. Incompetent fuckups, that's all you are. With your idiotic Sunday-school compassion. Go on, go grab some zzz's. By now I've got your number. I know you think you can get by by keeping your mouth shut. Get out of here. And don't think you can go out now. If I find out you went out I'll fix you good for the rest of your military service. Now scram. Reveille at eight.'

I was more stunned than hurt by that dizzying barrage. Dragging my feet, I took refuge in my room.

It was hot. The air was stale and sour; I opened the window. Down below lay a deserted alley sunk in darkness. The sounds of the city droned all around, sharper and more strident than those of the nearby station. My legs felt stiff but my mind was far from being able to sleep. Leaning on the windowsill, I smoked a last cigarette, trying not to think of what a nobody I was.

In the middle of the night I woke up, immediately gripped by a vague fear.

The light in the other room, still on, helped me make out the shape of a door, a closet. On tiptoe I leaned in to take a look.

He was asleep, elbows and knees in a chaotic jumble. Some kind of white covering was wrapped around the stump of his severed left arm. Without the protective shield of his dark glasses, his face was exposed as a mask of carnage.

The whisky flask was on the table, next to a vial. Sleeping pills, of course.

I coughed, banged a chair around. He didn't move.

Trying not to look at that face any more, I stepped into

the room. I saw a number of ties laid out in tissue paper in a box in the suitcase. At the bottom, underneath the shirts, a hard triangle. The revolver in its holster. Then, two bottles.

Behind me I heard his pinched breathing.

In the bathroom, his gear was all meticulously lined up along the edge of the sink: toothbrush and toothpaste, sponge cloth, cologne, a soap still in its wrapper, two brushes.

I sniffed the cologne, slipped a cigarette out of the box left on the table.

I felt petty and foolish, but also seized by a senseless, demented joy of spite and revenge. I did not, however, get up the necessary courage to open the package of new clothes. Next to the suitcase I saw his ID cards. I read the dates: thirty-nine years old. And the name: Fausto G.

I stood there for a moment, torn between the thought of making myself take another manly look at that face and the vain hope of erasing any memory of it now and forever.

I gave up the idea. Like a coward.

Back in my room, I sat down on the edge of the bed, the tasteless cigarette unappealing in the palm of my hand.

A steel-grey light was already faintly outlining the contours of the shutters. The double whistle of a train sank into the silence without a lingering echo.

I won't be able to stick it out all the way to the end, I thought from some remote corner of my mind that still remained alert.

I lay back down on the still warm pillow, my eyes closed.

4

With the tip of the cane he lightly touched the cuffs of the trousers, first one then the other, going slowly all round to the top of the shoe.

'Do they hang right? Short, maybe?'

'Perfect,' I replied.

He circled around. In the flood of sunlight from the window the linen seemed radiantly white.

With the dark tie, the glasses, his hand held stiffly against his stomach, he seemed unreal, a negative image of a photograph meant to mock the things of this world, to make them seem flat and remote.

He rolled his shoulders again, felt the edges of the sleeves from which the cuffs of his blue shirt peeped out.

'Sure I don't look like an ice-cream man? A nurse?' he stood stiffly, satisfied.

'It looks very good on you. Really.'

He made a face.

'Yeah. But a linen suit should be a little rumpled. It's the rule.'

He found the bed again, and lay back on it shaking his hips vigorously, stretching and bending his knees as he pedalled rapidly.

'How about now?' he said, back on his feet.

'It looks good.'

'That's all you can say,' he protested sceptically.

'But it looks fine. What else should I say?'

'Let's go,' he decided. 'You'll be glad too, without that usual shapeless uniform. Go on, go. Let's get out of here.'

'Yes, sir.'

He only appeared calm and cheerful. The sudden tightening of his mouth, the deliberate kindness in his voice betrayed his anxiety. 'A drink. Some coffee. And we're ready for anything.' He laughed as we waited for the lift.

A quarter of an hour later we were going up a narrow street that ran parallel to the port, lined with dark dank bars, cavelike shops, and eateries that smelled of burnt oil. On the ground, shrivelled greens and scraps of paper left over from the morning market; overhead a strip of sky angling between the profiles of the rooftops. Here and there a radio conveyed voices and music from darkened window openings. An old woman with a cluster of camera equipment started to step out of a doorway, studied us warily and in the end decided to remain under cover, hunched and twisted like a root.

'Anything?'

'Not yet. Only two. Hideous,' I replied.

'Maybe it's a bad time. People are eating. You think we're here too early?' he wondered.

It didn't seem like a real question; I kept quiet.

He stopped abruptly.

'Listen. I don't like this. It makes no sense,' he said. 'Find me a café. I'll wait for you. You scout around. Then come back and get me. Okay?'

'Maybe that's best.'

I left him at the bar of a café. Behind his cigarette he was sweating, as if his strength had given out.

'No haggling over money. And tell the truth,' he reminded me, his breathing still shallow.

I walked the whole length of the street, my pace quickening with the irritation that was spurring me on. From the precipitous alleyways that plunged dismally towards the port on my right, glimpses of a pale, distant sea could be seen.

Among the numerous cafés, I chose one from which loud blasts of music came; three or four girls appraised me as soon as I walked in. None of them seemed right. I waited until one of them made an overture.

Suddenly my irritation vanished, I felt practical and determined. Clearly I was resolved not to make a mistake.

'I'm telling you: she came down purposely. Her name is Mirka. The usual names. Her friend went to call her and she came down to have me take a look. She's waiting, right now. A doorway down the street, about twenty yards.'

'The one from yesterday? Are you sure?'

'Yes, I'm sure,' I lied.

'Okay, okay. Let's go.' He sighed wearily.

He didn't say another word until we had climbed up two flights of a very narrow staircase. Muffled voices came from beyond the walls.

'I had to promise her a bundle,' and I told him the figure.

He brushed me off with an angry gesture.

'Here it is. It's the only door,' I stopped.

'Just a minute.' He fretted anxiously; from his pocket he pulled out a white cotton glove that he quickly slipped onto his left hand, nervously smoothing each finger.

'Am I okay? Tell me.'

'Of course. Sure.'

'Not true. It's too hot,' he objected, frazzled. 'Goddamn handkerchief, why won't it come out? Ring the bell. What are you waiting for? Ring it.'

He fumbled, trying to wipe away the perspiration.

A woman opened the door, giving us a hard look. Her odour overwhelmed us.

'Will you wait here?' she said to me, pointing to the kitchen. Then, raising her voice: 'Barbara, where are you Barbara? Come and keep this fine gentleman company.'

I sat at a table in front of a shiny gas burner. Rays of sunlight struck the kitchen's metal appliances. I heard a thud from somewhere: it must have been him bumping into some piece of furniture.

An eye peered at me from the balcony, then the partial face of a shirtless little girl.

She came forward suspiciously, her thin arms clasped tightly behind her back.

'You didn't bring me any ice cream,' she said.

'I didn't know you'd be here!' I laughed. 'I'll bring it next time. Tomorrow.'

'That's what they all say, but if my Mama doesn't buy me ice cream I never have any,' she protested, pouting.

She rocked solemnly on her feet, then decided to trust me and came over to the table, resting her chin and fingertips on it. She smelled of talcum powder.

'In September I'm going to see the lizards. Did you know that?'

'Really?'

'Really. I don't tell lies.' She went on, 'In September

we're going away, to the seashore, but a sea that's far away, not this dirty one. We're going to a place with walls full of lizards.'

'Good for you. And what will you do with the lizards?'

'Nothing!' She laughed. 'You can't catch them!'

'Sometimes you can. Catch one, tie a string around it and take it for a walk.'

'You're silly,' she said angrily. 'Lizards don't let you tie them up. They're not dogs.'

'Right. That's true.'

'Don't tell Mama I called you silly. You won't tell her, will you?'

'No.'

'Cross your heart?'

'I swear.'

Suddenly friends, and to make it up to me, she began rolling her eyes, bobbing her head.

'If you give me fifty lire, I'll show you my scab,' she went on, lifting a knee that sported a Band-Aid.

'You shouldn't uncover it, otherwise it won't heal,' I told her.

'Today in the courtyard I uncovered it twice. For ten lire. But the second time a boy ran off without giving me the money after he saw it. I won't play with him any more.'

I lit a cigarette and she immediately ran around the kitchen fussing until she found a tiny ashtray.

'Mama yells if she finds a mess,' she explained, leaning her chin on the table again, 'and you know what she says? That men are all foolish bastards.'

'I see.'

'She says it all the time. All bastards. And another thing

she says: you're *Barbara* but when you grow up you won't need a *barber*. How funny.'

'That's a nice name: Barbara.'

'I like Maria better. You know what? After I die I'll be a Madonna. But the real Madonna, not a statue.'

She began scratching her stomach delicately with a fingertip.

'A mosquito bit me last night. Here. Can you see it?' she asked, sticking her tummy out.

'No.'

'Well, it bit me. When they bite me, Mama puts cream on me. It's cold; it makes me shiver.'

'Don't scratch it.'

'I will too!' She stuck out her tongue.

'If you do that you won't become a Madonna,' I said.

'I will too become one,' she protested stamping her foot, 'after I die. When are *you* going to die?'

'I don't know!' I laughed.

'You don't have a beard. You're not old enough to die.' She thought it over.

I reached out my hand to pat her, but she quickly jumped back.

'I'll perform lots of miracles,' she shrieked. 'As soon as I'm named Madonna, you'll see how many miracles I'll perform.'

'Good for you.'

'A hundred million miracles. I'll be clothed in gold and I'll have a hundred saints around me,' she continued, popping and rolling her eyes again.

'Sure,' I said.

'Those men – the bastards – though, I'll send them all to hell,' she concluded happily.

'Me too?'

'I don't know,' she said wrinkling her nose. 'You didn't bring me ice cream after all.'

I stood up and she immediately retreated to the doorway of the balcony.

'Are you leaving?'

'Not yet.'

I took a couple of steps to see if I could hear any sounds in there.

'The door is locked, the door is locked,' the girl chanted in a singsong, laughing.

'Right.'

'My mama always locks it when there's a gentleman. Did you come with a gentleman?'

'Yes.'

'Then you have to wait till Mama comes out. If you want, I can scream. She comes right away if I scream.'

'No.' I sat down again. 'We'll stay here and be quiet.'

She came back to the table, in a ray of sunlight that lit up the nearly blond stumps of her braids.

'Do you go to kindergarten?' I thought to ask.

'I go but I get sick. Every time I go I come down with a fever,' she said crossly. 'Mama doesn't want to send me any more. She says I'll stay with grandma this year. But I don't like that grandma. You know?'

'Oh,' I said.

'Yeah. I don't. She's old, all she does is pray, pray, pray and she doesn't understand. She never gives me any gifts. And she's always crying. Mama, on the other hand, buys me lots of dolls. Know how many? Guess.'

'I don't know. Let's see: ten,' I guessed.

'Fifteen!' she shrieked, laughing. 'Nobody ever guesses,

nobody. Fifteen. One that's very big, bigger than me even. She's dark-skinned, all black, but I don't like that one and I don't count her. I never sleep with that black one.'

I heard the sounds of running water, the hum of words; the woman appeared with a sigh.

'Go out to the balcony, Barbara,' she said.

'No, I won't,' the girl retorted.

'Would you like some coffee too?' the woman offered without looking at me; she was already bustling about the gas burner. 'Tell me, that friend of yours, he's a bit nervous. With you, does he talk?'

'He's just strange,' I replied.

'Strange all right, poor soul, him too,' she said screwing the coffee-maker together. She had big hands and pale, unpolished fingernails. 'Still, he's a gentleman. Say whatever you want, but he's a gentleman. And loaded: I mean, rich. Barbara, go out to the balcony.'

'No,' the child replied sullenly, shaking her head. 'I'm staying here. Right here.'

'Go or I'll call the wizard!' the woman hollered.

She had a powerful behind; her arms were rosy and plump as they slipped from her dressing gown. Taking her time, the girl retreated to the threshold of the balcony.

'I don't believe in the wizard any more. Or in the witch. I don't believe in them, no I don't!' she shouted and stood there open-mouthed.

'And you, young man, won't you stay with me a little while?' The woman turned around and smiled, her dark eyes always appraising. 'Ten minutes, okay? Or are you ashamed because of your friend?'

'Not today,' I said embarrassed.

'Whatever you say. You're making a mistake though, another poor fool. But I'm not the type to insist.' She laughed tiredly. 'Here's your coffee. With this contraption all you get is a cup and a half. Is half enough for you?'

'It's fine, thanks.'

'I'll take his in there. If you're not staying, then leave quickly. And you, Barbara, you'll be sorry if you move or shout like before. No television tonight if you do.'

From the doorway she turned, lowering her voice: 'But he wasn't wounded in the war, right? Too young. What, then? Well, it doesn't matter, it's this lousy world. Why doesn't he get married? He must have a nice pension, I imagine.'

Before getting up I tried waving goodbye, but the child, peeved, slammed the glass door and stared at me from the balcony without waving back.

We walked for a long time; he was indifferent to the heat, his face turned upwards, the bamboo cane no longer held out ahead, but clasped tightly under his arm.

I didn't feel like talking. Every so often I was amused by the hasty way people anxiously made way for us on the sidewalk, hugging the walls closely. We strolled around a large rectangular piazza with a skimpy park in the centre. My mind was blank; even the noise of the traffic drifted off without bothering me.

I remembered the revolver in the suitcase with a sense of lethargy: just as long as he didn't shoot himself during these few days with me. Who the hell knew what was going through his head?

'Why don't you get married?' I asked when we were seated with a couple of ice creams.

'What?' he answered coldly, irritated at being ambushed, though he quickly regained his composure. 'What's got into you? Are you out of your mind?'

'I was just asking. It would be logical.'

'Logical?' He sneered, showing his teeth. 'Bullshit. Get married. You sound like my cousin.'

'I don't see why not.'

'Love isn't polenta. Get married and then you'll be happy. Better to get married than hang yourself,' he continued mockingly. 'You're just like my cousin the aunt: she lives on proverbs. But she's seventy years old. Aren't you ashamed of yourself?'

He had settled the cup of ice cream between the slightly curved fingers of his left hand, now stripped of the white cotton glove. He stopped stirring it with his spoon.

'Just my luck to get an antiquated, conventional conformist like you,' he said.

'I'm not antiquated. I think logically. Or at least I think I do. That's all,' I replied.

'You think, ergo you're annoying. It would be better if you were missing a cylinder,' he laughed drily. 'I would have preferred the usual illiterate, or at least a bizarre type. But no: instead they saddle me with a thinker, who as soon as he opens his mouth comes out with a hundred gaffes.'

I chose to just take it. At a table nearby two guys raised their heads over the straws of their soft drinks, listening intently.

'But the world is full of nice women,' I went on.

'Really? You keep them. Enjoy yourself.' He cut me off without lowering his voice.

'There's no need to put an ad in the papers to find the right one.' I didn't feel like holding back.

He was rolling a still unlit cigarette nervously between his thumb and forefinger.

'You say that because you've seen me act soft in the head,' he said then, choosing his words. 'Think what you like. Feel free. If it matters, I'll tell you that those types of women have always had that effect on me. We were better off with the brothels. But you: you can't possibly have any idea. What a country this is! Completely laughable. Nothing works, so what do they come up with? Shutting down the bordellos. The country's only real salutary institution.'

The two guys at the other table were sitting sideways to look at us. They laughed.

'You know why I haven't yet killed myself?' he asked.

'No, sir.'

'Because even if I croaked it wouldn't bother anyone!' he shrieked shrilly. He quickly added, 'This ice cream was disgusting. As soon as you get outside of Turin, forget desserts. Not even a decent beignet. Write that in your journal.'

'You won't ever die, sir,' I said.

'What's that?'

'I know it sounds stupid. But that's what I think. I can't explain it. I don't think you should ever die,' I said, confused.

'Nice compliment. A fine wish.' He laughed, disconcerted. 'You're not jinxing me, are you, Ciccio?'

'I saw the revolver,' I said softly.

He started.

'Yes, sir. Last night. You were sleeping. I looked in your suitcase and I saw the revolver.'

He nodded, his face tightening. 'Dirty bastard,' he murmured.

41

'I'm sorry I stuck my nose in where it didn't belong, but I was right to,' I said defiantly.

'Filthy traitor. Rotten swine,' he went on, controlling his harsh breathing. His right hand grabbed the edge of the tablecloth and twisted it into thick folds.

'Call me whatever you want,' I defended myself, trying to overcome the tremor in my voice, 'but I'm not sorry I did it. I could even be held responsible if something happened.'

'You have no responsibility. No right. No nothing,' he shouted coldly. 'I'll beat the living daylights out of you. I'll kick the shit out of you.'

'You do whatever you think is best,' I tried again. 'But I'm not your orderly. Or your lightning rod. I can't put up with everything.'

He allowed himself a faint smile.

'You'll put up with it,' he said, pronouncing each syllable, 'you bet you'll put up with it. I'll make sure you're raked over the coals. You have only one way out. Know what it is? Run off. Scram.'

'I'm not the type.'

'You are. Idiot. Go ahead, get up. Get out of here. Beat it. Let's see that courage of yours. I swear I won't start shouting. I won't run after you. Girlie.'

He waved his cane. The two guys were now staring intently at us, unsure whether to give us an amused smile or a look of pity. The cane dropped back on the table.

'Go on. What are you waiting for? Move. You think you're needed? You're more useless than a dead weight. Get lost.'

'I wouldn't do such a despicable thing.'

'It's not despicable. It would be courageous. A word you've never heard of. What you like is saying "yessir". And snooping around on the sly like a thieving servant. Well? are you going or not?'

'No.'

'I know what you're thinking: you'll go when it's convenient for you. That's what you're thinking.'

'Whatever you say, sir.'

He laughed in short, harsh bursts.

'Poor fool. I'm a thousand steps ahead of you, I am. So watch out. I might be the first to scram. And force you to trot behind me with your tongue hanging out.'

I didn't say another word, torn between the nagging thought that I had gone too far and the bitter satisfaction of having finally managed to speak out. He went on waving his cane, his breath laboured.

The two guys stood up. Before leaving, they gave us a long lingering look. I gave them a rude gesture, which persuaded them to move off into the park. I heard them laughing in the distance.

'We should go back to the hotel. For the suitcases,' I decided after a while.

He stood up. We started walking along the street at a rapid pace again, unable to find a single word to say.

I was very tired. My head felt flushed and heavy, but I got by without slowing down. His arm under mine now sought to lure me back into the usual hopeless pity, but I managed to remain detached, to resist, even though I was ashamed of the confused reasons for such absurd resistance.

At a very crowded crosswalk we bumped into one another, but no profanities or rebukes were thrown at me. I was in no mood to apologize.

The city's noises had grown, rising into a long, protracted

rumble. The late afternoon air grew even denser, scorching hot, despite the impending evening, its electricity quickening everyone's steps and gestures. Along a stretch of arcades I realized I was staring hungrily at several large, colourful film posters: a grainy, hazy shape of a woman with a machine gun against the swaying yellow light of a rich pagoda.

He was whistling, lips tight, chin thrust out. Then he stopped, shaken by silent laughter, which he stifled in his chest.

The sound of a siren at the port made its way through the walls and the muffled depths of the city.

In the bar back at the hotel he perched on a stool and began drumming on the counter with his left hand, silently outraged at the lack of service. The last of the sun poured through a window, glinting off his dark glasses and lighting up his forehead, his hair.

'Beat it,' he told me as soon as he was able to bend over a glass of whisky. 'I'm staying here. Until it's time for the train. You: fuck around wherever you want.'

His hand was trembling. He drank the first sip with barely controlled craving. The wrinkles in his linen suit scrunched along his back.

I sank into a chair in the next room, by this time indifferent to any poster images.

5

... Maybe it's all because of my low self-esteem. Idiotic and pointless to try to fool oneself: therefore I must predictably blame my modesty, that is, my mediocrity ... Otherwise I would have known: even his most absurd words, vicious, hostile, would have managed to stir something in me, real intelligence or real rebellion. Not pity, because pity alone comes and goes and is of no use, but a different way of looking at the world, at life: seeing it and seizing that life in its most enigmatic senses, and laughing at it, laughing at the good and bad in it, with it, as he can, albeit atrociously ... Maybe I'm just a poor, miserable individual who scrapes by on the piddling, presumptuous stash of his reasoning and doesn't even enjoy the impulses, good or bad, of youth ...

That's what I was thinking, as the train plunged along in the night, he asleep in his corner, his head bowed, wobbling as the seat shook, his right hand in his lap. He had drunk too much, up until our departure time, and took some pills as soon as we boarded the train.

Violent whistles from the front of the train broke the dark silence of the night.

I watched him with the utmost care, marvelling up and down at the scars and pockmarks on his face, the impeccable knot of his tie, the slim wrist of his right hand, the lithe firmness of his crossed knees. Even the motion of the train added to his degree of gracefulness, rocking him with subdued languor, and I realized how that gracefulness constituted a perfect shell for the desperate fury that lay within it.

I envied him, in some obscure way, for the effect he had managed to create of himself.

His merciless words, that attitude of contempt, were then abruptly overturned in my mind and I finally saw how funny they were, so slyly charged with diverse tones, really laughable. I clamped my mouth shut to contain the burst of laughter that surged in my chest.

Who knows what his everyday life is like? I thought, in that house, with his cousin, the cat, the corridor, the whisky in the cabinet. But it seemed impossible even to guess. I couldn't imagine him, picture him, on some street or piazza or the Lungo po, Turin's river walk. Maybe for him too this trip meant a temporary escape from a limbo of routines, trapped one inside the other.

It seemed miraculously blessed not to know.

I went out into the corridor; the dark glass reflected me as a vague silhouette of uncertain contour. Leaning at the window I tried to peer into the night, a black void that for a split second suddenly fractured into shadowy walls, poles, signs, deserted gates slashed by vivid lights, and was then quickly restored.

In the reflection of the glass, my forehead pressed against the pane, I saw my eyelid, shiny and dark, the grain of the skin enlarged, the eye's moisture quick to reappear after each blink.

And I remembered him in bed at the hotel, without his

dark glasses, the gaunt, livid, turbulent splotch of his face against the pillow.

I had eaten. I had convinced myself not to wear my uniform. The new suit continued to console me, and now the surprise of that earlier, furtive laughter made me feel good.

I thought about something nice to say to him, later on or the next day in Rome. Maybe a special kindness would make things easier for both him and me. I couldn't think of any particular words or gesture, but that vague determination was enough to cheer me up.

Kindness, yes, or even some humour: that's what I should stick to, to make our trip a pleasant one.

There were few passengers on the train, just two or three in each compartment and almost all of them asleep. A solitary woman at the back, an elderly lady with an open book. The smell of old dust, of newly oiled door handles and other hardware was not unpleasant. We would stop twice more before Rome, arriving there in the early morning.

I avoided looking at my watch, content at feeling suspended within the protective shell of the journey, by the idea of the city to come, in that silence that freed you of any obligation. I promised myself I would write at least two postcards home from Rome.

Turning, I looked at him again, motionless in his corner, his right hand closed around the glove on his left, his chin nodding in submission to the train's rocking. Everything seemed right, elevated to a higher order.

He awoke at a more abrupt jolt, his hand immediately searching for his cigarettes.

'Hey there, Ciccio. Still hanging in there?' He yawned. 'You didn't sleep much.'

'I made a mistake: vitamins, not sleeping pills, damn. I must have had too much to drink.'

'I'll say.' I laughed.

He laughed too, swallowing to get rid of the bitter taste of sleep in his mouth.

'What about you? Get any sleep?'

'No. But I'm fine. I even ate. There are just a few people. It's quiet.'

'Almost too quiet,' he agreed.

'Are we staying long in Rome? Nearly two days have already flown by,' I asked.

He sighed. 'Who knows? I have a cousin who's a priest. He writes to me all the time. I should drop in. Have we passed Pisa?'

'Not yet.'

He made another face to cleanse his tongue and palate.

'A mint. That's what I need. Since I don't have one . . .' he said taking the flask out of his pocket. Then, but politely this time: 'You take a sip first.'

'Thanks.'

Intersecting beams of light cut through the thick darkness. Perhaps we were nearing Pisa. A train passed us sending back vivid blasts of colour.

'Once I had a girl with enormous breasts. Like pumpkins.' He muttered, pretending to be sullen. 'While we slept, she would turn around and routinely give me a K.O. with one of those things of hers. What a life, can you imagine?'

We started laughing. He drank again, held the bottle out to me, and when I handed it back he did not put it in his pocket.

'And a colonel of mine? His own words, I swear: during

the war, in Africa or Russia, I don't remember, as a lowly lieutenant heavily in debt because of poker, he always volunteered for the most foolish missions. For each mission there was an award. Cash: ready for him to get his hands on immediately, if he came back alive. He was scared to death, but without poker he would have dropped dead even sooner. And so he managed to get two silver medals and a promotion besides.'

The train slowed up as it neared Pisa. The night shattered into slivers of light that eventually began to glide alongside us more closely and systematically. Amid the gloom of a valley, a large reddish smoke plume from a foundry or cement works made the ridges of the hills appear harsh.

'Yeah. That's how life should be.' He sighed, relaxing reluctantly, a tremor on his lips.

The gentleman who got on at Pisa had a new suitcase. He was tall, elderly, with white hair. He sat down and gave us a polite smile before leafing through the newspaper.

'We have a visitor, Ciccio,' he said.

The gentleman looked up, gave a broader smile over his newspaper.

'I noticed the compartment was nearly empty,' he said mildly. 'But if I'm disturbing you . . .'

'Heavens, no!' He laughed. 'Make yourself comfortable. Want to have a drink with us?'

'Pardon?' the other man murmured.

He held out the flask.

'I said: do you want to have a drink with us? Are we or are we not in Tuscany?' he tossed back in an even tone.

'Well, ah, really . . .' the man said, quickly summing us up.

49

'Look, I think you've more or less emptied your bottle. Thank you. I wouldn't want to . . .'

'Impose? Please do,' he said leaving him no way out. 'There's a reserve in the suitcase. Oral ammo. Twelve-year-old labels only.'

The man thanked him again, took the flask, held it in his hand a moment, warily winked at me as a sign of understanding, then handed it back with a thank-you.

'Truly excellent,' he added.

He took a sip.

'Well. A cheat,' he then pronounced.

'What's that, sir?' I said.

'We have a cheat at our side. Yeah. Maybe he thinks he can put one over on us. Watch out, Ciccio.' He laughed sadly.

The man gave a slight start but did not respond. He went back to his newspaper.

'Don't let him get away, Ciccio. Otherwise, with the excuse that we're drunk, Mr Cheater will run off.'

'All right, sir.'

The man refolded his paper, doubtful and troubled, then tried tapping a finger against his temple, his eyes questioning. I shook my head no.

I had to accept the flask again and drain the last drops.

The gentleman had just started to stand up when he grabbed him with his right hand forcing him to remain seated.

'Please. My dear sir,' – he laughed – 'you wouldn't want to deny this human piece of wreckage here a little conversation, now would you? You, Ciccio, stand at the door. That's a good boy.'

I slid the glass door of the compartment shut and leaned

against it. I was just a little foggy, but with a kind of urgency in my body, itching for a brawl, some words, some action.

The seated man was prepared to be tolerant. His butter-soft face focused.

'Were you in the war?' came the question.

'Of course. Ethiopia and later . . .'

'Not me. Just peacetime for me.' He laughed, abruptly raising his gloved left hand up to his face.

There were beads of perspiration on his lip.

'Forgive me,' the man began, 'I greatly respect your condition. I wouldn't want . . .'

'My condition? What condition? Do I have a condition, Ciccio?' he interrupted the man.

'What I mean is, I understand. Believe me. I'm old enough to have seen the world and to realize that . . .'

'An Italian old enough. Who knows what a filthy swine he secretly was. Right? Without hesitation. Presto!' He laughed.

But the laughter immediately froze on his lips as he drew them into a pitiful grimace.

The man again sought support by looking over at me. I shrugged and gave him a wicked grin. Every move I made surprised me with its promptness and arrogance. The smell of whisky tickled my nostrils.

'Listen, sir,' the other man went on, 'I don't know you and I'm sorry. If you will allow me . . .'

'You're not allowed.'

'I only wanted to introduce myself,' the man responded meekly.

'And I have no intention of knowing your useless name. Too bad for you if you say it. Be anonymous. It suits you!' he shouted.

With some difficulty the man recovered a ghost of a smile and tried to change the subject. 'Excellent. Well, let's just say: I feel like I'm in a real night-time adventure. A little something unexpected doesn't hurt.'

'Ciccio, the gentleman is asking for something unexpected,' he said. Then: 'You, Anonymous, have you met Ciccio? Known as the terror of the two seas.'

He moved closer until he was just a few inches from that pale face. The man straightened up and backed away at least a little.

'I'm drunk, your Excellency.'

'That's fine. Quite all right,' the gentleman rallied. 'Every so often it's just what's needed. A release. I always say . . .'

'Not a thing. You don't say. You can't say.'

The man leaned back against the seat, trying hard to regain a modicum of breathing room. He was sweating, his wrinkled eyelids quivering without their normal control.

'I'm the one who's going to say something. Know what it is?' he threatened. 'That we're in a rotten country.'

'A rotten world, for that matter.' The man laughed shrilly in a burst of relief.

'Granted. But above all a rotten country. Where your rotten breed is more clueless than anywhere else,' he shouted.

'Now I understand,' the gentleman nodded. 'You're not Italian, and so . . .'

'Me, no. That's right. I'm only from Turin,' he concluded, tired.

His chin was wobbling spasmodically. His right hand slowly flailed about before he was able to get a few more words out. He shrank back into his corner.

'Raise those fine flags high, so they don't pick up the stink on your hands,' he breathed with some difficulty.

He appeared wiped out.

The gentleman began to rise cautiously, quietly took his suitcase and newspaper, then went out to the corridor, quickening his pace at once.

He handed me the empty flask, pointing to the suitcase. I climbed on the seat and rummaged about, shuffling things in confusion, until I found the other whisky.

'Go away, Ciccio.' He coughed, his fingers uncertain as they struggled with the metal cap. 'Go and have a proper conversation somewhere else. Aren't there ever any girls on these goddamn trains? For you, I mean. I need to sleep now.'

'We had a good time,' I said.

'Huh?' He looked up for a moment, his smile bewildered. 'Yeah.'

'He ran off quicker than a rabbit,' I tried again, 'like the conductor yesterday. This guy too: who knows what he'll have to say about this trip?'

He made a vague gesture, writing it off in the air.

'You open it.' He held out the flask.

'Wouldn't it be better if . . .'

'Please,' he suddenly groaned despairingly. 'Open it. And that's that. No preaching.'

I unscrewed the cap and handed back the flask; he clasped it with his hand against his chest. 'Still here? Go on, go. Beat it. I have to try and sleep. That's all. Don't give it a thought. Please.'

I went back into the corridor. In the surrounding darkness, streaks and glimmers of a first tenuous light appeared.

Every spiteful urge had left my body, seeped away; a bland sense of peacefulness soothed my muscles and my thoughts.

Soon the countryside would unfold in feminine undulations. Maybe I would see horses and long-horned cattle wandering loose among the patchwork of fields. And conical haystacks topping gentle slopes.

The two syllables of the word *Ro-ma* rolled on my palate like a precious morsel of great sustenance.

I no longer had the heart to turn around, to spy on him in there.

6

The storm was still spewing out brief bursts of rain, but the lightning and thunder were moving off. From the window of the hotel I saw a parking attendant dash across the street, stooped under a makeshift cellophane poncho. He hunkered in a doorway, where the legs and shoes of people who had already squeezed in to take shelter could be seen. Every so often a girl would lean out, laughing, to take a look. The ochre walls showed large splotches of rain; the pavement and a lop-sided row of rooftops were crossed here and there by channels of silvery coils, vivid purple streams.

A colourful umbrella rocked slowly on a balcony, a final gust of wind overturned it.

'You haven't read me the horoscope yet, chief,' he complained from the bed.

In the grey light, the room's decrepitude – the threadbare curtains, the now faded flower-patterned panels above the doors – was fully exposed. The bedsteads, unmatched, were of iron. The staff, after quite a long, trying telephone call, had granted us a shabby partition which was now placed between the two beds, further reducing the space and light.

'Oscillations in the business realm, be cautious when

buying and selling. Relationships: turn the other cheek to an offender. Health: psychophysical balance,' I read.

'They should be hung,' he grumbled. 'Go on: Capricorn.'

'Great ambitions are not suited to you: take all ideas that come to mind with a grain of salt. Relationships: remain calm. Health: don't overdo it at work. Why Capricorn, sir?'

'Because of my cousin the priest,' he scoffed. 'Still raining?'

'It's almost stopped.'

'Too bad. Roman thunderstorms: they hardly last. Wait for me downstairs. Have them call a taxi. I'm going to deal with this pain-in-the-ass cousin.' He started to get up from the bed.

'Wouldn't it be better if I waited here?'

'Don't be silly. I've known this fleabag for an eternity. Nothing ever changes here. Not even the holes in the carpet. Go downstairs.'

His plate of sandwiches was still almost full, the bottle of Saint-Émilion, on the other hand, was empty.

A group of elderly American women crowded about the second-floor landing. They wore plastic caps and their feet were covered in transparent bags. They laughed as they moved around and regrouped, examining small flasks, a colourful scarf, some painted seashells. The doorman was elderly as well. Extremely tall, he seemed to be supported by invisible crutches; with a finger he directed his assistant, a staunch, mustachioed young man in a new uniform.

The taxi kept us waiting.

When he came down, the old doorman immediately went towards him, his arms rising like wings. They shook hands and exchanged a few words with brief, thin smiles.

Then he stepped outside to gulp in the freshly washed air.

'Filthy old goat,' he said cheerfully. 'He must be at least a hundred. If he likes you, you can ask for the moon. Otherwise there's no tip big enough.'

High clouds raced along swiftly revealing patches of sky; the smell of rain and wet rubber tires rose from the sidewalk.

The taxi driver turned down a narrow street and then another at high speed. The bamboo cane descended on his shoulder.

'Unless you have hot pepper up your behind, slow down,' came the rebuke.

'Of course, sir. If it's okay with you, it's okay with me,' the man laughed. He had a big toothless mouth and the back of his neck spilled over his collar in a huge roll.

We sped along the river, the waters murky with a stale covering of foam. The leaves of the trees still seemed weighed down by the rain. After crossing a bridge, the taxi cut through a square, took an uphill street.

'It would have been better to leave you at the hotel. Or let you take a walk. What do you have to do with my cousin the priest?' he said.

'But I'm glad to come.'

'Suit yourself. *De gustibus*,' he said unenthusiastically. 'Not that he isn't likeable. On the contrary. Young. A font of knowledge. Still, he's all priest.'

'A little holiness is always good for you,' the taxi driver offered.

'Bravo,' he leaned forward, ready, 'and you know what I think? That to become really holy every Italian and his brother should come to Rome with permission to strangle a Roman. Am I right?'

'Well,' the driver laughed uncertainly, 'you mean Ministers or actual Romans?'

'Optional. Whoever comes along.'

'Rome is magnificent,' the man objected with a grim sigh.

'Magnificent and deceitful,' he said.

'I'm ignorant and I admit it. I'm no match for you two,' the driver replied, sizing us up in the rearview mirror. His jaw was working as he spoke. 'But I've got my own ideas. And they're clear.'

'Listen to that.'

'That's right. But I've learned to keep my mouth shut. Out of propriety. So I don't open it any more.'

'Better your mouth than your eyes, chief,' he said icily.

We came through a jumble of crooked houses in glaring colours, divided by strips of gardens, a few trees, pretentious painted gates. The church at the end was low and new, of pale stone, with a minuscule bell tower. The churchyard was dry, as if it hadn't rained there.

'Do you really want me to come? I could wait here. There's even a bar,' I said.

'A bar? A miracle. A quick coffee: to cleanse our voices before the holy water.' He brightened. 'Why wait here? You'd better come. He might go crazy and want to hear my confession. Then how the hell would I get out of there?'

The handkerchief-sized vegetable garden behind the church was a joke, with stretches of gravel where tomatoes could have been grown, and pots of cacti planted in the ground in no order whatsoever. There was a painted bench against the wall and a wrought-iron table; a large geranium plant lushly overflowed its container.

'Let's sit out here,' the priest invited shyly, 'it's cooler. Did you hear about the big storm? Here though, only a couple of drops. It's always that way.'

He was tall and lanky; they resembled one another.

The first exchange of greetings, questions, had evaporated with a faint laugh or two, the priest's cheeks reddening unexpectedly.

He moved his cane until it brushed between his knees.

'Hey!' he said. 'No cassock any more?'

'No, no,' the other said hastily, 'I wear the cassock too. But I only wear it when I'm traveling. You know how it is.'

'I don't know a thing,' he responded. 'How come? Are you ashamed?'

The priest blushed again.

'No. It's because of people. I look young, so they don't think much of me. Better to avoid the issue.'

He turned to me, squinting a little. 'And you, don't call me Father or Reverend or Reverend Father. Call me Fausto. Like him, yes. We're nearly twins, you know. And address me informally.'

'Easy with the twins,' he corrected. 'I'm an Aquarian, you're a Capricorn.'

'Still there's only a difference of maybe twenty days or so.' The priest smiled.

'According to your calendar. Not according to the constellations.'

The priest laughed again, more faintly, constantly wringing his hands in discomfort.

'Damn. Look where I find you. You wrote to me from a college, months ago. You've regressed to parish priest, or am I wrong? Weren't you a scholar? What happened?'

An elderly woman in a flowery hat came forward, crunching on the gravel, and set down a tray. A bottle of water, three glasses with a squirt of mint syrup.

'Thank you, signora. See you tomorrow. Thanks for everything.'

'Well, I did as you asked, Reverend. There is nothing prepared. Do you want me to stop at the dairy shop? It will only take a minute,' the woman said.

'Thank you, signora, I'll take care of it. It doesn't matter. This is fine. Good evening. See you tomorrow,' the priest said, flustered.

'Who is she? The housekeeper? And you call her *signora*?'

'Quiet. Be nice,' the priest whispered anxiously. 'She's a good woman who helps me a little. She lives nearby. I don't have a housekeeper. I have to get by on my own.'

'A first-class establishment. Congratulations.'

'Come on. Be nice. I'm the one who asked to return to a parish. Nowadays it's important to act, more so than think.'

He had a quiet, humble voice, with sudden wobbles and high notes.

We drank. The taste of the mint was too sweet and the water almost warm.

'I don't hear any chickens.'

'Fausto, what's the matter with you?' The priest laughed, bewildered. 'What chickens?'

'A parish rectory always has chickens. At least a housekeeper and some chickens, am I right?' he persisted. 'And I don't hear any here. Where the hell have they stashed you? Are you being punished?'

'But I just told you that . . .' the priest replied, quickly giving up with a sigh.

'It's beautiful here,' I offered.

'Oh yes.' The priest immediately shook himself. 'And at night I have all of Rome spread out below me. A sight that never ceases to amaze me. Oh, I'm sorry, Fausto.'

'Sorry for what?' His reply sounded calm. 'I don't give a damn about Rome. For me it's the capital of Turkey.'

'You never change!' The priest laughed with a hand over his mouth. 'How happy I am to have you here. God bless you, you never change.'

'You have, however. You did something. I'll bet on it. You can tell me. Otherwise they wouldn't have kicked you out and buried you in the boondocks like this.'

'Buried? Kicked out? Why do you say that?' the poor man fussed in a weak voice. 'I'm happy here. I'm finally happy. I'm useful. A person can study and study, but it's just ambition. The problems remain, humanity is still out there waiting. So one might as well make himself useful to his fellow man. I'm sorry: I can't explain it very well.'

'You explain yourself, all right. But you're talking real nonsense. Be useful. Humanity. Fellow man. The longings of a spinster. At this rate you might as well end up in the country as a pastor. But a privileged pastor with a full belly, a farmstead, a loft full of salami, and so on.'

The priest hid his face in his hands as if to wipe away some kind of fatigue.

'Do you want to know something, Fausto?' Then he said quietly, 'I envy you. I've always envied you. You'll say it's blasphemy, but here's what I think: that you're fortunate because your suffering is with you, every minute. It stimulates you. It liberates you. Make me stop, please, don't let me keep talking.'

'No, go on, continue.' He took a deep breath. 'Say it, say it.'

'Are you sure I'm not hurting you? I wouldn't want to . . . If you only knew, I've thought so much about it during these years.'

He was trembling slightly, his hands anxiously fussing with his cheeks, his temples.

I thought of standing up, but the gravel would not allow me to steal away in silence the way I wanted to.

'Go on. Keep talking.' He laughed quietly. 'Nothing can upset me any more. At this point: talk.'

'Don't say that.' The priest was sad. 'I know you. You try to defend yourself with that arrogance but instead . . .'

'Instead? Say it.'

'I don't know. I don't know anything any more.' The priest seemed to give up. He was very pale. I could see the shadows under his eyes quiver in a web of tiny veins.

His voice burst out as if he were trying to convince himself.

'I think your cross illuminates you. So be it, it may be your reason for living. That is, for salvation. You're saved. That's why I envy you. Because you've already been pardoned. I envy lunatics, idiots, the sick, innocent children. Only they are able to see and understand. More so than I can.'

He had lit a cigarette and was smoking, letting it dangle from his lips.

'Do you believe in the devil, cousin?' he then asked mildly.

The priest shrugged his shoulders faintly. His hands left his temples so he could rub his eyes.

'You don't know. Right.' He went on without removing the cigarette, his profile stony. 'And yet you should believe in him. As long as the world was afraid of the devil everything was different. There were good demons and bad demons. Cops and robbers, in short, the old story. Am I making sense? Once the bad guys were gone, even the good guys had no face. The devil disappears, and all at once miracles disappear. Am I wrong?'

'Good, Fausto, good,' the priest murmured.

'You'll say I'm talking like a simpleton but . . .'

'These are the very subjects that are the most difficult. That make us uncomfortable,' the priest parried.

'But if you envy me so much, I can help you out: I have a gun back at the hotel,' he laughed mildly.

'Please.'

'Of course being blind is certainly fortunate,' he conceded, meticulously stressing every word. 'You know why? Because you can't picture anything any more. At least that's what happened to me. I can't imagine or even remember. Great advantage. A diabolical advantage, almost. If I could see the world again, here right now, I would only look at rocks, deserts. Not even trees or animals. I too am a rock. Would I be saved and pardoned for this, in your opinion? Listen: sometimes my darkness is happy. I swear. I'm quite content in it. Rare, but it happens. It's hard to explain. Okay, that's enough now. You see? I too have done some thinking. It took a bomb in the face to make a captain think. Am I talking too much? But you, if you have such a great desire for martyrdom, pick up and go to Africa. The world is full of Africas and Cottolengos. Purposely made to save and console your tormented souls.'

He flicked the cigarette butt away with a twitch of his lip.

'My Africa is here. My Cottolengo is here. You just have to understand things. Look around. If you only knew . . .

Don't let me say any more. I shouldn't tax my strength like this.' The priest sighed.

Cautiously I tried to turn around on the bench at least to get them out of my sight for a moment. Up above, the sky was very clear, an expanse of almost phosphorescent blue. The hum of the distant city was barely audible.

'Why don't you come to Naples with us? Turn the key and disappear for two or three days,' he said.

'I can't.'

'Sure you can. We'll have a good time. Here, I'll even give you a moral alibi. A friend is expecting me in Naples. You know, the one who had the accident with me. Him too, blind as a bat. Come with us. You can console us. Preach to us. Attend to our sins. And we'll reciprocate with vermicelli and clams. How's that for an idea? Make up your mind.'

'It's not possible. I can't leave here.'

'Mass and confessions?'

'Hush, please. Let's not speak about these things. The confessions: they're devastating.' The priest hid his face.

'Imagine that. And here I thought they were amusing.'

'That's enough Fausto, please.'

He whistled a refrain through his teeth, lit another cigarette.

'Okay, okay, I get it.' Then he said, 'I thought by now you were all modern, on the ball. Instead, just listen to you. You suffer, you have a mystic, old-fashioned soul. At least try not to think too much. It turns us into furious beasts. Don't you have a parish recreation centre here? Children who come to study catechism, to play ball? You know, those priest things of yours.'

'Not yet. It's a new parish,' the other straightened up a little.

'You could start a school.'

'I tried. Maybe in October I'll try again,' the priest replied briefly, wearily. 'And you? What will you do when you get out of the military? Get married?'

He was looking at me, perhaps regretting the earlier intimacies. His clear gaze widened to overcome his shyness.

I didn't have a chance to respond.

'Ciccio is unattached. Footloose and fancy-free. That's all they dream about today. Freedom. What do they think it is, freedom without money,' he said in a cloud of smoke.

'If you're free, you'll be alone,' the priest stressed, no longer looking at me. 'Get married, young man. As soon as you can. It's still the most sacred thing. Life: life is divine.'

'And those who study too much go crazy. So our elders said,' he scoffed.

'Your father. Such a good man. So upright.' The priest brightened tenderly.

'As upright as you want, but please, what a caustic, witty streak he had in him,' came the quick retort. 'I remember one day, I must have been ten years old, a woman came into the pharmacy. Disconsolate, clinging, distrustful as only certain peasant women can be. She said to my father, "Sir, my child won't eat any more, he doesn't play, he doesn't laugh, he doesn't ask for anything, what should I do? He has no fever but isn't there some medicine perhaps?" And my father, standing there sternly with his thumbs in his waistcoat: "He doesn't laugh, doesn't eat, doesn't ask for anything, doesn't play? Oh what a phenomenon, throw him under a train, quickly."'

'Fausto!' the priest gulped pitifully, trying not to laugh.

'That's how it is. Not just stories. Now that's it. Don't you have any hard liquor? Any kind. That mint, I swear it depresses you.'

He stood up and we were at his side. I as usual amazed at how he managed to get his bearings in a flash, remembering the gravel from before, his cane ready to discern and touch the corner of the geranium box.

The priest accompanied us as far as the churchyard.

The roofs and stone of the houses began to soften in the first tender shades of violet.

'Right around there, a taxi stand,' that faint voice advised us.

'Do you still write those little articles of yours?' He turned to face him again, the cane aimlessly twirling in the air. 'I've never been able to read them, of course. But I know they were important to you. Even the magazine hasn't come for some time. My overly devout cousin can't figure it out. For her you're a pure genius.'

'No. That's done. It's over,' the priest replied with some effort. 'They were just frivolous vanities, trifles.'

'Or they've censored you.'

'What a thing to imagine,' the priest evaded in a whisper, his eyes wandering over the deserted square. 'It was ambition. Presumption. I thought I knew. Then I realized it.'

'You mean some bishop of yours graciously illuminated you. With a currycomb.'

'For heaven's sake. Don't be mean.'

'Why not? I'm so good at it. Oh, the hell with it!' He flared up. 'I'll throw you in my will. If I don't nibble away at them first, which is mathematically certain, a few pence will be left to you. That way you can ditch the habit.'

'Fausto, please . . .'

'Once you discard the habit, what do you find?' he continued relentlessly. 'That you're just one of a billion cases of nervous breakdown due to exhaustion. Am I right?'

I looked at the priest, a little embarrassed. His forehead was creased with anxiety. He no longer looked at us, his gaze remote.

I realized that with every ounce of strength remaining to him all he wanted was to see us go away.

He held out three moist, feeble fingers without returning my grip.

Their embrace was tepid and silent.

'Is he gone?' he snarled immediately afterwards, slicing the air with his cane. 'An emergency whisky. Drastic treatment. Damn you, Ciccio. You didn't open your mouth. Some help you were.'

'He was so pathetic.'

'Pathetic? Right. What a ninny.'

We crossed the church square heading for the bar.

'We have to eat a good meal tonight,' he decided after a stroll through the piazzas and parks of the city centre.

Under the trees we stopped to listen to the soft hoofbeats of horses galloping on a track. A blonde girl rode by a few feet away, gleefully whipping her foam-covered horse.

We were now walking up a wide street with cafés and restaurants, I was describing them to him in minute detail one after the other, not forgetting the lights, the waiters' jackets and glances, the faces and figures already sitting at the tables.

'At the end, on a corner, there should be a certain bar with large comfortable armchairs. One hundred and thirty brands of whisky. Heaven!' He smiled contentedly.

We had let ourselves flow along with the crowd on the sidewalk, in a surge of gentle indolence. The expanse of sky, the profusion of colours, the dark lush border of a distant garden got under my skin, making me feel more alive and raring to go.

I found the bar. It was quiet and sombre, with those same armchairs, but he wanted to sit outdoors, where he had a great time discussing alembic still blends with an old waiter. Indulgent words and ironies flowed in an exchange of flowery expressions.

Then: 'Let's get out of here. No frou-frou restaurants tonight. A plain old hole-in-the-wall trattoria. With guitars. Just what we need.' He was enjoying himself, weighing his glass.

A glimmer of a smile gave him the affected air of a portrait from the past.

'Do you really think you're a rock? That's what you said before.' I put our familiarity to the test.

'Of course not. I never think. That's the secret: don't think about anything, just laugh. All one big continuous laugh. Don't get tedious on me, Ciccio.'

He flicked the ash from his cigarette with a sweeping arrogant gesture.

'But did you really want him with us in Naples, your cousin the priest?' I persisted.

'Oh my God, I said it while knocking on wood. What am I? A good deed doer?' He drained his glass with relish. 'Still: if I really wanted to do a charitable deed I should fire a shot into that cranium of his. A sure thing. In the state he's in, the unfortunate bastard, it would be a liberation. Don't you think so?'

'No, sir.'

I was prepared to endure his laughter or some type of scorn, but strangely enough he responded with a carefully considered, wary tone of voice.

'You're right. Then too maybe it's all pretence. Not that he's putting on an act, the poor reverend. He doesn't realize he's pretending. But his suffering is still in his mind. You, of course, don't believe in the soul. Whether it exists or not, it's certainly not the soul that does us harm.'

7

It was Sunday. I wasn't surprised at his decision to put off our departure until the following day. As he coughed, leaning over the sink, I read the newspaper out loud. First the important headlines, the horoscope, last of all the classified ads in the health and beauty section which listed the addresses and phone numbers of prostitutes. At certain exaggerated adjectives, allusions to lavish attention, luxury and confidentiality, the welcome to buzz the intercom any time from 10 a.m. to 11 p.m., he would straighten up from the sink racked by wheezing laughter, immediately stifled by renewed coughing.

He stepped out a moment, half hidden by a large towel, to tell me, 'Don't worry. I don't feel venereal today. You won't be forced to associate with risqué company.'

He was extraordinarily modest. He would withdraw to the bathroom even just to put on or take off his shirt. He always deftly managed to conceal his left arm when it wasn't covered up. And his tie: he could knot it in three moves.

'Don't you want me to read you anything else? Politics?'

'What does politics have to do with me? Does it guarantee me the end of the world? No. So that's enough.'

From the bathroom he dictated the morning's plans: first

a barber, then a walk to the zoo, finally an outdoor restaurant.

'Provided we don't come across a sung mass. Don't you love them? To me they seem perfect. Even without being able to understand the words.'

I had slept too much. The hot, still air kept me from shaking off that heavy feeling. The acidic wine we'd been drinking in a tavern until late the night before was turning my stomach sour.

Outside, the angle of the sun was brutal. The stones reflected too much light. The ornamental work on a house throbbed painfully in my eyes. The desire for Rome, the sense of opulence enjoyed the night before, had been spoiled, turned to toxic fatigue in my body.

'C'mon, walk. Good God! Let's go, buddy. Stand up straight. You feel like a limp rag,' he prodded me.

The avenue stretched straight ahead of us glazed by the sun, with tall, slender trees along the sidewalks. It was deserted, just a few clusters of young people scattered in front of a café, their mocking voices raucous. The houses followed in a row, all the same, their windows shuttered. The bamboo cane clanged blithely against the shutters over and over again.

'And I complain about Rome. Bastard that I am. Nothing but jealousy. It's open to you, Rome is. Feel it? Barbarian or not. What a day. Good for the soul,' he said impulsively.

He settled down in front of the lion cage. Gentle gusts of wind raised clouds of dust from the paths. Beyond some shrubs, the outlines of taller cages could be seen. From a pine tree came the shrill screeching of birds.

He took a deep whiff.

'What's he doing. Sleeping?'

'Every now and then he opens one eye,' I told him.

'He doesn't stink,' he said resentfully, 'and what I really like about animals is their gamy odour.'

He nudged me with his elbow, handed me the cane.

'Try to stir him up. Get him angry. Christ, let's hear you!' he commanded, irritated.

I held out the cane, shook it a few inches from the bars. The lion opened its jaws wearily without even breathing. His upper lip fell back slowly, docilely over his canines. He lowered his head again, winking.

'He won't budge,' I said.

'Goddamn world. I bet they stuff them with pills in this place. They must even kill off their fleas with flea-powder,' he said angrily, stamping his foot. 'That's why he's just lying there like a prick.'

There wasn't a soul along the path. The squeals of children reached us from afar mingled with the barking of seals. A yellow balloon rose up above the treeline, floating in the sunlight. I stood, flung my arms wide, let out a cry. The lion, bored, slowly looked away.

'What time do they feed him?'

'It says 11.30.'

'Too late. I want to hear him now. Right away!' he objected.

I kicked at the wooden railing that separated us from the bars; I tried to lean closer. The lion shifted his haunches with deliberate voluptuousness, his head motionless, his gaze lost in space.

'Big?'

'Big, yeah. Male. With a dark mane. From Kenya. His name is Sam.'

'Fuck,' he muttered.

At a corner of the railing were two signs with descriptions and warnings.

'I'll give you a good whipping, Sam,' he threatened through clenched teeth.

He leaned forward just a little, his right hand firmly on the railing, brandishing his wooden glove.

The lion shifted his gaze from his distant target, and stared at him with a first quick gasp. From the depths of his lungs he drew a viscid breath that gradually grew into panting, his black eyes flashing.

In a bound the lion was against the bars, his mane bristling. He roared, bits of straw hanging from his pale belly, his claws slashing the air ferociously, only to end up grating on the iron.

'Friendly. You see?' He calmed down immediately, nodding happily at the groans that now rumbled forth, muffled by the animal's agitated pacing.

'Smell that? You can even smell his odour now.' He sniffed.

The lion circled around two or three times, panting, before curling up again in the most remote corner of the cage, his teeth still bared.

'Let's go,' he took my arm again. 'Of course the gorillas are more easily riled. There's nothing like the gorillas.'

'Spaghetti for you. Then stuffed octopus. For me, meat. Meat soaks up the whisky,' he decided.

'I've never eaten octopus,' I objected.

'All the more reason. Hungry?'

'Yes, sir.'

The restaurant was nestled in a corner of the piazza behind

a low green hedge. A very fat, sweaty waiter stepped among the empty tables, moving sparingly. Heat hung in the centre of the piazza; red dots flashed before my eyes.

'And afterwards? What would you like to do?'

'Anything is fine with me,' I replied.

'Want to go off on your own? See a movie?'

'I don't know, sir.'

'Bravo, Ciccio. A born tedious bore. Never an idea. Can't ever make up your mind, huh? C'mon. It's Sunday. Show some spirit or this time I'll punish you.'

I started when he banged his glass down, making the table shake.

I saw him tense up, his whole face alert and rigid. He gestured with his right hand, but only after a long moment was I too able to perceive the distant tapping.

Across the empty square an old blind man with a white cane appeared, his torso upright but his legs a little wobbly. He wore a straw hat and a garland of coloured tickets that hung from his neck down to his waist. Under his arm was a folded chair. He crept forward through the empty expanse of white stone like a fly in an overturned glass.

'Do you see him?' he asked coldly.

'Yes.'

'Yes what? Explain. What is he doing?'

I described the man to him. Meanwhile the old man had reached a corner and was gingerly feeling around. Two or three times he tapped his cane on the sidewalk ahead of him, but very lightly, soundlessly. He stood still, then began turning halfway around, his face and eyeglasses turned up towards the sun, his shabby hat not even shading his forehead.

'Dressed decently?' he asked.

'Fairly.'

'Now what is he doing? Is he moving? Is he leaving? Say something, damn it. Don't sit there in a daze.'

'He's sitting down. He unfolded his chair. Now he's sitting there. He's lighting a cigarette.'

'Jesus F. Christ.'

The waiter was watching us. He made a move as if to come over and say something, then decided not to.

'Go on,' he said tensely, still cursing, as he pulled out some folded notes, 'buy those lottery tickets from him. Every last one. Hurry up. Make him go away.'

'What should I say to him?' I asked, mystified.

'Take them and pay him. Got it? And for God's sake open that mouth of yours and speak. Are you asleep on your feet?'

I got up heavily and to my surprise saw the waiter join me halfway across the piazza. We crossed that wasteland with our heads lowered, he grumbling a few foolish words about the heat, and that deserted Sunday hour.

He explained it all to the blind man, while I waited a few steps away with the bills in my hand. The old man's face was white as a candle, his lips ready to pull back in a broad toothless smile. The waiter helped him fold his chair back up and relieved him of the garland of tickets. Sticking the money in his pocket, he directed him along the wall, all the time teasing him gently about that shameful surfeit of good luck. The blind man laughed, bewildered. After a few yards he stopped, his face turned towards the sun and the piazza, the greenery of the little restaurant opposite, to raise his hat in a slow ceremonious salute.

We returned to the table in silence.

'You did a good thing, sir. A virtuous deed,' the waiter

said. 'That man is unfortunate in more ways than one, if I may say so. When he goes home without any money, his wife beats him as well.'

'You don't say!' He laughed happily.

'A monster of a woman,' the waiter added, wiping his sweat with a napkin. 'She takes care of him, dresses him, but if he doesn't earn anything during the day, she beats the daylights out of him. They live right behind here. We know them well.'

'And him. Does he ever fight back? Just takes it and says thank you ma'am?'

'He fights back all right. Poor man. With a bottle.' The waiter laughed softly. 'Capable of downing seven or eight litres a day. He's certainly not going home now, you know. If he gets back too early, she sends him out again with more tickets. It's greed that devours her: because they aren't really poor. So he goes to the church. To nap where it's nice and cool. He's shrewd. He comes back here in the evening after supper.'

'And drinks!' He was having a good time.

'When he gets here he's already loaded. His wife doesn't deny him his wine,' the waiter continued. 'The wine is how she keeps him on a leash. Anyway: a good deed, what you did. Given what the world throws at us nowadays.'

He sized us up with a long look, clearly meant to make out the possible degree of our kinship.

'I'll bet one of these days they'll find her strangled to death,' he said.

'The wife? You think so?' the waiter mused.

'We're evil. We blind guys.'

The other protested with a calm smile.

'Don't say that, sir. We all know that it's the hand of God.

And why evil? It's ignorant people who are evil. Would you like a nice cup of coffee, afterwards? Top quality, as it should be? I'll bring it myself.'

'Stick those tickets somewhere. Under the tablecloth, maybe.' He then muttered half-heartedly, already bored. 'What a drag. Being kind is so tedious. Stifling.'

The afternoon seemed to go on and on.

He didn't want to go back to the hotel. We strolled through the desolate streets, angling here and there in search of some meagre shade along the walls. Every so often an unexpected glimpse of a familiar Rome would recreate a flight of steps, then another narrow street vanishing into the distance and the high overhead greenery of terraces suspended from the sky by a thread, but I had to move on quickly, his firm arm hanging on mine, the blistering Sunday ready to swallow me up in new avenues, boulevards, enormous traffic circles flattened and scorched by the sun.

Later he decided to sit down at a café near a fountain, the roar of the water violent and monotonous. At a table nearby some guys were gesturing and shouting loudly in a heated discussion over football. Players' names and insults clashed fiercely in the air, then dissolved in pauses of oppressive silence. The shapes of motorcycles parked along the sidewalks glinted. The umbrellas cast skimpy circles of shade. The surface of the table felt fiery under my fingertips.

He went on at length about the water, about how noisy it was but as though out of habit, without any real enthusiasm; each sentence immediately obliterated by the next.

I looked at that fountain, its copious chalky whorls, the streams that plunged down raising bits of greenish foam. It did not give off any coolness: my jacket and shirt were stuck to my back, my shoes had a film of dust. But strangely enough he hadn't yet complained about the heat.

Around us, closed shops, faded nameplates on the walls. Someone peered out through the crack of a shutter. A man on a bicycle approached very slowly, got off, and with weary gestures carelessly threaded a chain between the spokes of the wheel before disappearing into a doorway.

'So: do you have at least one friend? Or not? Someone, anyone? Something to talk about? Were you born in a cabbage patch? You never say anything about yourself,' he suddenly protested.

'How do you always manage to guess?' I asked, amazed. 'The very instant I was telling myself: say something.'

He nodded, but without any self-satisfaction.

'One of my virtues,' he went on. 'For example, with me: are you a friend? Be sincere, otherwise it's pointless.'

'Yes. I think so. Why?'

'Whys and wherefores.' He shook himself irritably. 'Why all these whys. Be direct. In short: do you feel like a friend? Do you feel that I'm a friend? Or would you rather be sitting with those others back there, talking about Boniperti and Rivera? Go on, tell me: it would only be natural.'

'Of course not.' I laughed nervously.

'Do you feel different from those guys?'

'A little. Not better. Just different.'

'Exactly. Aside from football, do you feel comfortable with yours truly? Yes or no?'

'Sure I do. Really.'

'Bah!' he made a face. 'Let's hope so. Look, friendship is a serious commitment.'

I swallowed my usual 'why?' What came out was: 'Meaning?'

'Meaning that sooner or later, or maybe even never you understand, I could ask you to do me a big favour. Big but possible. Nothing impossible.' The voice was only a little sad.

'That's fine, sir.'

'That's fine, sir.' He mimicked me, the tension in his face finally relaxing. 'Of course I don't demand oaths. Your word is enough for me. Fair?'

'Fair.'

'I must say you're not totally mute. A syllable or two does slip out occasionally.' He laughed.

I was embarrassed. 'But I have so many things to say, in my head. They just won't come out.'

'Poor youth!' He sighed, though distractedly. Then: 'Let's get out of here. Did you notice? A speck of ice in the whisky. Just one. That's always the way in these tight-fisted joints. Let's go back to last night's bar.'

He was already on his feet. His scrawny sunlit figure cast a lengthy shadow into the street.

'You liked that bar too.' He started walking, grabbing my arm. 'All in all you're a well-bred gentleman. Boy-oh-boy, are you! Why hide it? Your father: what's he like? And you really don't have a girlfriend? Tell me.'

The lights began to dim one after the other until the packed room went dark. A waiter moved about with a flashlight, casting exploratory white circles around us. Then even the flashlight went out.

There was a sharp smell of disinfectant in the stuffy place; I had my back against a rigid wall of wood and velvet. I felt his elbow nudge me.

'Now what?'

'I don't know. Nothing yet,' I replied.

'Are you having a good time?'

'Actually not really, sir.'

The glowing ash of two cigarettes rose and fell. I heard them laughing softly beside me, him and the girl with the rustling outfit. She had sat down at our table, her eyes knowing, her throat, shoulders and breasts like cream. We were drinking champagne, dubious glances thrown at us from remote corners. The total blackness all around us now provided a minimum of respite to ease my embarrassment. An isolated round of clapping broke the silence at the bar behind us. I had watched two strippers and a magician's act, describing them to him in a whisper. The magician was an old man with a wrinkled face and painted smile who had finished his routine by balancing at least twelve quivering doves on his shoulders, hat and hands. The stripteasers had hurried through their numbers with quick, grudging moves. Only afterwards, when they left the bar and formed a wide semicircle to study us, did the creamy creature come to sit at our table, laughing and winking, chattering in broken Italian.

The clapping resumed, loud and overly enthusiastic. In the darkness I was aware of the velvety slide of the curtain.

A burst of piano music quickly rang out and at the back of that dark funnel-like space three phosphorescent little skeletons began to dance. Even the outlines of the top hats on their skulls glowed brightly. Disjointed shinbones, kneecaps and shoulders danced happily in sync to the rhythm of an old fox-trot that became more and more frenzied. Lightly they followed one another's lead, barely touching, their steps crossing, the skulls rigid to provide balance. Suddenly the piano betrayed them by switching to a tango: the skeletons frantically and chaotically bumped into one another, vertebra entangled within vertebra, their top hats about to fall off. A last angry comic scuffle disentangled them in the proper arrangement, order was restored and their new steps were smoother, pelvises gently swaying in slow measured undulations, top hats in cadence. Then the music stopped: the illuminated stage broke the spell and a young man with Indian features wearing a black coverall stood behind the three limp puppets. Responding with a shy smile to the scant applause, he bowed slightly and ran off.

'The only Italian she knows is swear words. As usual.' He laughed, leaning back against the wall. 'Good-looking, right? A heifer from up north. Listen. Give her a try. She won't bite. Go on. Stuff you won't find on the Monte di Pietà.'

He weighed her breasts lightly in his hand, delighting in fake sighs, the girl's eyes quick to scrutinize mine before laughing and shaking him off.

'I am very hungry, no? Fillet? Yes, the fillet. Please,' she said wiggling around.

She laughed without showing her teeth, that childish voice of hers far too affected.

'I would have bet on bandolero steaks, the ones marinated in rum or bourbon.' He continued to be amused, his fingers nervously tapping the table.

The waiter arrived with the fillet and more champagne, while on stage a black woman with an oiled body undulated among flaming torches. From the top of each torch black paraffin smoke curled upwards.

We had already deposited our bags in the luggage room

at the station. We were to leave for Naples early the next morning.

'This one here doesn't get off until four a.m.,' he said.

'So what good is she? If we have to leave.'

'She'll come to the station with us. That's what. Finally somebody to see us off,' was his ready response.

As soon as the lights dimmed, the girl moved closer to him, whispering in his ear. But maybe they weren't words, just delicate breaths, and he basked motionless in that fragrant surge.

'Here they'll rob us. Like fools,' I had said to him from the beginning.

'So what? It's fine just the same. Believe me. Or maybe you're embarrassed.'

'What does embarrassment have to do with it? I just think it's dumb,' I said angrily, an impassive waiter close by.

'So then, what else should I deny myself, in your opinion?' he retorted mildly. 'As for the money, you're right. Another minute of this life and I'll end up right in the poorhouse. But we'll think about that later on. Okay with you?'

I had taken his arm, avoiding the attentions of the waiter. We had descended into that darkness, the sounds of the music suddenly louder.

Now his elbow nudged my ribs again.

'Hey, Ciccio. Know what she's thinking about? A handbag. She says it only costs a thousand Swiss francs. Some bargain. Watch out: you're holding the money, that's what I told her. It seems the handbag is sold in a shop right near her house. Of course you'll miss the train. Right? Don't tell me you haven't thought about it.'

The girl was watching me, a smile quick to appear and

reappear on her face, her gleaming gaze intent. The waiter had brought a small plate with four apricot halves in syrup. She lifted one with a spoon and gently, bit by bit, slid her tongue slowly in and out of its depression, her eyes half closed, avoiding mine at first, then suddenly staring at me, at the effort I was making to meet her eyes. The champagne was going to my head; my eyelids felt heavy. By this time the girl had decided to swallow the apricots languidly, pouting.

After a while she went back to the bar. The show was over. Two or three couples danced, dragging themselves listlessly onto the stage, now transformed into a dance floor. A veiled light revolved, drawing and erasing pink and blue shadows. I saw them bring two coffees to the table. I drank with some effort. The air had become toxic. I thought I spotted the magician's profile among the disorderly crowd at the bar. Older, his wrinkles powdered, perched on a stool, he was playing dice by himself, a big sandwich in his left hand. Even the black woman from the torch act sprang out of the darkness for a moment to have a drink, looked around, alone, disappeared before my eyes.

To hold out, I clung to his voice, breathing heavily as he told a story. He seemed to have sagged between the table and the wall, his left arm flung out in abandon, his right hand clutching a cigarette. In the changing flashes of light his face had lost any sense of definition.

' . . . in this cave, holy God. Always in a cave. Who knows how they manage. To work. To live. Blind, yet they work, they reproduce. You see? Insects, I'm talking about. I've been talking to you for an hour, Ciccio. What's up? Are you sleeping? Feel nauseous? Insects. How do I know? Once I called information, I swear. How could I make it up? I never learned to read with my fingers, not me. No rehabilitation, I told them right away. There's nothing left to rehabilitate, nothing to learn, my dear medical professors with all those fucking degrees of yours. So then: the nice, kind voice of that girl on the phone. How she laughed! She always seemed cheerful. The patience she had. Naturally she must have been pretty ugly, to be that patient. Can you believe it? She read half the encyclopedia to me on the phone, explaining about blind insects who work and so on. In the dark. The mole cricket, for example. A carnivorous cricket that eats worms and digs tunnels. It lives at night. He and his missus are causing serious damage to the agricultural crops, you know? And then there are the worker termites. Less appealing though, since they're asexual. Not only blind but asexual on top of it, thanks to mother nature's just reward. They work, they build, they sweep, they gather food. They even cultivate edible mushrooms, I swear! Check it out if you don't believe me. While their good queen oversees them, grows fat, eats mushrooms and produces forty thousand eggs a day. She doesn't work there any more, that girl. The times I called her, afterwards. Damn her and her shitty kindness. Or maybe she got tired of it. Maybe she asked to be transferred to another office not to have to listen to me any more. I can understand it. What do you think?'

I don't know how he managed to drag me over to the telephone. The magician was watching us as he kept moving the dice up and down a green-felt tray. His doves, I thought dully.

A sulky bartender dialled the number and indifferently handed over the receiver.

'What do you mean, night? What night? It's morning.

Don't you think it's time you went to Mass? Confess your sins?' he shouted raucously, irascibly, happily to his cousin the aunt. He held the receiver away from his ear to allow for the sighs and querulous cries of the frightened voice on the other end. 'Of course I'm fine. Just dandy. You won't be coming to my funeral. Nor will my cousin the priest. Saw him today. A tiresome bore, him too. Call the Baron for me. I know he's sleeping in my bed. I want the Baron. Now. Hey, Baron, is that you? How are you? Speak up. Go on. One little purr. Come on, handsome. There's my good fatty. Of course you know who I am, it's me, come on now precious chubby boy. You'll give me a nice purr now, won't you? Come on, precious. Or I'll cut off your whiskers, you know. Are you embarrassed because of my aunt? Tell me. Let me hear you. No? To hell with you too, then.'

He hung up, his hand trembling. The bartender had poured two small glasses of a dark liquor.

'Courtesy of the management,' he said grimly.

I didn't even try to refuse. He drank, and immediately afterwards found my glass too by feeling around.

'Herbal,' he decreed coughing.

'An extract. Very digestive and stimulating, sir.' The bartender wasn't surprised.

The magician had turned away, I saw his curved back, the faded pattern on his jacket.

'How about we wake up my cousin the priest? Just a thought. Maybe he needs us. We might manage to get him to come to Naples with us. Having a priest along could be useful.'

'For heaven's sake, sir,' I replied, though I realized that I could not offer any opposing arguments.

'He's a good man, the little priest. He's amusing.' He began complaining in a fake voice. 'You, Ciccio, on the other hand, are a nobody. A cipher. Why can't you manage to keep me company?'

The bartender's putty rubber face lost its frown in a faint smile of complicity.

'You're not a friend,' he went on. 'You don't speak, you don't sing, you don't wag your tail. Where the hell are you from, *madamina*? Because you're a little bit of a coquette, like a *madamina*. Or does that offend you?'

'No, sir,' I said patiently.

I kept my hands on the bar to steady myself; I felt the wood grow damp under my palms. The bartender poured a third glass of liquor. I ordered myself to say no with my head to display a modicum of authority on my part. The man nodded, took back the glass.

An insolent, early light hung over the houses when we went out. In three taxis two men slept sprawled out between the seat and the steering wheel; a third was reading the newspaper.

'Rotten bitch. It wouldn't have cost her anything to come with us,' I heard him rattling on. 'But she's no admiral's daughter. These goddamned whores always say they're admirals' daughters. Never understood why. You didn't say a word to stop her, Ciccio. You're too befuddled. Did you see her again afterwards?'

'No.'

She was right there, walking along, not twenty yards from us, her tender bare flesh unharmed by the light of day. She climbed into a car, went past us, elbow raised to shade her eyes and forehead.

'Incurable provincial captive that I am.' He coughed. 'If things go on this way I'll be talking to myself any minute. The nut house. Trips, not on your life. I should have myself taken to the blessing of the animals. Ciccio, why don't you shove me under a tram?'

He could hardly stand up, his shoulder leaning on mine, his knees caving in. Every now and then he tensed up to repress a shudder.

'Naples and death,' he began repeating, continuing on in the taxi, saying it over and over again non-stop and coughing as we hurtled through the deserted streets and piazzas to the station.

I fell into a kind of absurd calculation of the days already spent and those yet to come. The fizz from the champagne was bubbling in my stomach in troublesome eruptions. I gave up on the intricate cabbala concerning time and held my breath, suppressing hiccups.

A large fountain circled around us, its water steely-grey; he stuck his head out the window to drown in that air, that cool sound.

Then: 'The Baron, too. Even him now. What would it have cost him to say something? He always talks to me on the phone. He gets angry, he gets offended, but then he always mutters something. This time, nothing. More spiteful than usual. You think it's my fault, Ciccio? Am I really such a bitter pill? And to think I see myself, I consider myself a poor canary blinded so he can sing better.'

He laughed shrilly, only to have it turn into laboured gurgling. He bent over, pressing his stomach.

'What was that last drink? Manure? Do your guts feel rotten too?'

Darkness obscured my eyes, ripped into my throat. I struggled not to come apart. I kept my eyes fixed on the door handle trying not to look elsewhere, not to close my eyes again.

The taxi driver braked rudely, dumping us off in front of the station without a word.

'A shame to leave here. Too bad we can't stay. But on to Nero's!' he cried, swaying along, his cane raised.

Only the patience of a porter extricated our bags from the luggage room. Overturned cups and saucers in the sink at the bar, the raucous thumps of voices from the loudspeakers drilled into my skull.

'Istanbul. Calcutta is where we should go. Forget Naples. Only three hours' sleep. What an eternal idiot I'm turning into. May God strike me dead.' He went on protesting in the train, his lips livid. He had already swallowed the sleeping pill.

Huddled miserably in a corner, I tried to shield myself as much as possible with the edge of a curtain. I felt the light, now too strong, pressing and prying between my eyelids like an incandescent blade. Cries, shouts, noises tore brutally around us.

'Relics of ourselves. That's what we are, Naples and death,' he continued muttering, a dark, swollen vein in the middle of his forehead. 'Is anybody in here?'

'No one, sir,' I said.

The train began to move.

8

I saw them at the back of the terrace in the marble-veined evening sky. They were speaking almost listlessly, with long intervals of silence and not a shadow of a smile, he, upright as a post as usual, the other, his back already curved, though he was tall and stocky, straining to hold himself erect. They seemed out of place against the vibrant stripes of a large umbrella.

'I'll say goodnight. It's late for me. Do you need anything? By now you know where everything is, you've seen everything. Make yourself at home. See you tomorrow,' the soldier said from the door. He had the narrow face of a weasel, with unexpected flickers of cunning, and smooth hands. He had first said he was a student, then a records clerk, but his tone was that of someone afraid of saying the wrong thing.

I remained alone in that enormous room crammed with portraits. A last glimmer of light shone on the face of a woman surrounded by an oval antique frame; the pale flower pinned between her throat and shoulder stood out starkly. Groupings of photographs edged with silver lay on a desk, small tables, mantelpieces, a piano.

In the afternoon the soldier had shown me around the house, a maze of hallways, cubbyholes, rooms one inside the other. From almost every window you could see views of the city plunging down to the sea, precipitous and unruly, like a chaotic crèche.

I would be sleeping in the room of a maid who had left on vacation just that morning. The drawers and closet in the room had been emptied or locked, the walls were bare with damp, branched shadows. There were no sheets under the bed cover.

'Good thinking, that too. Four men in the house, or at least you three if I really don't matter and no one counts me, and what does he come up with? He sends the only useful person, the only woman, on a trip. Who hadn't even asked to go. The proverb is right: the brains of those whom God hath marked work differently. See what you can do. Mind you, I've already decided: I'm eating at the barracks. Beds, brooms, dustmops – as far as I'm concerned, they can wait until Christmas. I'm not an orderly. You neither. If they have an itch, let them scratch it,' the soldier had promptly told me.

'What's the name of your guy?'

'Vincenzo V. But just call him Lieutenant. That's enough for him. He retired as a captain, but he insists on still being called Lieutenant. Naturally: those brains I just mentioned. Still, a person with heart, a whining bore but good-hearted. Believe me: I've been here six months now. And thank the Almighty God, at least he has both his hands. How does your guy manage to shave? Do you see to it?'

I saw them on the terrace, still standing side by side, their cigarettes lit. They had ironically felt each other's stomach and abdomen but with quick, almost disgusted touches, neither one laughing. They weren't talking any more.

I had managed to rest a few hours. My exhaustion and all its various toxins had vanished, but I still felt gripped by a strange, indecipherably hostile force, like a cobweb, or better yet perhaps, a soap bubble that had enclosed me: rising higher and higher, uncontrollable, swaying, it was carrying me away, every aspect of the world increasingly diminished, cold and distant.

I too went out on the terrace, taking care to retreat to the corner farthest away from those two.

The city was already all lit up, a dense undulating jungle of lights and lamps, multicoloured patches that ran up and down the gulf's coastline in a blur of loops and scallops, swirls and eddies, beneath a sky streaked with purple. At the point where the purple darkened, a cloud was slowly forming the head, then the shoulder, and finally the prodigious hand of a giant. The last curls of his hair still caught the sun from below the horizon. Rising towards him from that jungle was the thick growl of an immeasurable beast, stretched out, sleepless, humming from millions of pores, orifices, scales, wrinkles, recesses of its skin exposed to summer's inert vapours.

My prison felt tighter and more oppressive, and I immediately felt an urge to dive in – not walk, but actually plunge in among those lights, that breath, and disappear there.

They moved and crossed the terrace in silence, shoulder to shoulder, the white cane and the bamboo staff swaying in sync.

The lieutenant had a deep thick voice given to sudden dubious languor; his guest's words abruptly interrupted what he was saying. Three, four times they retraced those few feet in a straight line, the host's bald head gleaming like an eggshell. They didn't appear to be friends; they never displayed a sincere gesture of affection, of understanding.

The lieutenant said softly: 'I have the courage. But I'm so afraid.'

His response was laughter that stung like a whip.

Prudently I returned to the living room, preferring not to listen to their talk.

Through the windows, in the room's darkness, I could still see the sea, black and obscure, surrounding two large vessels whose masts were illuminated like perfect triangles.

Finally I decided to move, to at least try to find the light switches.

After supper the girls arrived. Two were daughters of the owner of the nearby restaurant where we had eaten, and two were their friends. They were very young. The one with glasses laughed and was more active than the others. They immediately moved about the house as if they knew it by heart, finding glasses, bottles, ice, some feather pillows in a closet.

They followed one another back and forth between the kitchen and the living room with loud cries.

'Ines Candida Michelina Sara. You're driving me crazy,' the lieutenant complained from the depths of his armchair. 'Where are you running to? Why are you fussing around? Here, all of you come here right now. Sit down.'

He, already shielded behind his whisky, was silent, as if oblivious to it all.

'You too. Say something. They waited so long for you, poor girls,' the lieutenant prodded.

'Women. By now they're grown women. A far cry from

the little girls of four years ago. I can barely stand them,' he grumbled.

'Fausto,' the other gave a long sigh, 'we might come to an end, but not the world.'

The bespectacled Ines appeared, manoeuvring a fan with its long electrical cord.

'How about a little air? It's stifling in here. Come on, don't start drinking like sponges right away, otherwise we'll leave. Would you like another cup of coffee? Is the breeze too strong?'

She lowered her voice then and moved to the two armchairs, where she said quickly, giggling, 'Did you notice, Fausto? Sara is still in love with you. Really head over heels, poor girl. Like when she had braids, remember? She even bought a new perfume today. French. Say something to her, Fausto, make us laugh.'

'Ines, you gossipy mischief-maker, you. A fine friend you are. Be quiet for once. And call the others. What are they doing over there?' the lieutenant objected listlessly.

'They're embarrassed!' Ines laughed again before running off, leaving the fan on the floor.

'Well. They must still be virgins?' he said lazily.

'Captain, have you lost your mind?' the lieutenant said in alarm, shocked. 'How can you talk that way. Four fine young women worthy of respect. I'm even Candida's godfather . . .'

He gave up with a hopeless wave of his hand.

'Curiosity. Just talk.' He yawned. 'What do you expect me to think? They're women, so talking is useless. You have to touch them.'

'Fausto,' his friend scolded him again, 'don't you remember

four years ago? When they accompanied us to cafés, to the park, and we bought them ice-cream cones?'

'Baloney.' He was quickly silenced.

They came back in together, their eyes focused on me, as if weighing my possible though not yet established complicity. They sat in a row on the sofa in front of the two men, nudging each other, making faces and smiling, their giggles quickly muffled by their hands across their mouths.

'Be good now,' the lieutenant warned.

He didn't have many scars on his face, just a reddened zigzagging slash behind his right ear. His dark glasses made his large head, that fleshy nose, seem even heavier. His chin wobbled at the slightest word or collapsed in a trace of a double chin.

'Any ideas, girls? Let's not stay up too late though,' he asked around mildly.

'A game. Yes, a game!' Ines cried immediately.

She had taken off her glasses. They all seemed indifferent to the soft, warm cushions, to the dozens of eyes looking down on them from the whiskered men along the walls, from those garlanded matrons and dames in their frames, with their prodigious chests, painted mouths, tight curls at their temples.

I saw Sara reach out her fingers to touch his right hand as it gripped the glass.

'Do you have a headache? Do you need anything? Some ice?' she asked, her wide eyes enormous in her small, pale, too round face.

Her girlfriends on the couch silently made fun of her, mimicking her with puckered lips, their eyes half closed.

'No, no,' he replied, abruptly moving his hand away, the

mechanical twitch of an annoyed smile playing at the corners of his mouth.

'A game, a game!' the others now shouted, though studying their friend with avid suspicion.

'No screaming. Mother of God, please, my head. A game, as many games as you want, but quietly. Otherwise that's the end of it. There's a play on the radio tonight. Be good or I'll go to my room,' the lieutenant implored them, his limp hands moving around in space.

'What game do you want to play, Fausto? You decide,' Sara asked softly, leaning over intently.

He laughed, his shoulders immediately assailed by a shudder: 'The only one there is, by God. Blind man's bluff.'

We had moved out to the terrace for ice cream, the night air hot and humid.

The pistachio-hazelnut cream had melted in the refrigerator; we drank that sluggish glop from glasses after dousing it with whisky.

'Remember how often you used to dream? Do you still dream?' Sara's voice was cautious but determined. 'Once you told me that you had heard an animal under the bed. Running. Small. Orange-coloured. Some kind of rabbit you thought. Or maybe an armadillo.'

'Armadillo. What the hell is that,' he retorted tonelessly, 'I don't remember a thing.'

'But Sara does.' Michelina's voice was sweetly ironic as she paused a moment with the tray of empty glasses. She was tiny, quick to show her teeth, and she had chubby knees. 'Sara is like a bad conscience. She remembers everything; she never rests.'

'Don't be catty.' The lieutenant sighed from afar. He was stretched out in a wicker lounge chair, having relinquished any desire to control the evening.

'Ciccio!' The gloved left hand went up.

'Right here.'

'Good, don't go anywhere,' he said wearily.

Sara looked at me as if seeing me for the first time, with a faint sad smile, her hands clasped under her chin. Her nails were well trimmed, but she had gnarly fingers that she continually tried to hide.

'Why don't you take off your jacket? With this heat,' she spoke to him softly, 'don't you want to be more comfortable?'

'How silly you are,' he replied.

'Next year I'll be at university,' she tried again.

'And your sister?'

'Oh, Candida will do just fine as a cashier at the restaurant with my mother. She's good-natured. A girl who will soon marry, poor thing.'

'Why poor thing?' He laughed.

'Because she's a worthless creature, "made out of nothing", God help her.' Sara's reply showed some irritation at the hopeless bother of that conversation. 'Whether she marries a head cook or maybe even a grand pasha, it's all the same. It all goes back to that.'

'And you're not like that. Right?'

'Me? No. Of course not!' She was suddenly animated, her hands clenched. 'Fausto, you haven't even asked me what I'm going to be studying at university.'

'I bet you'll tell me just the same.'

'Rude and impolite.' She laughed, though nervously. 'Well: medicine. Happy?'

'Should I be? If I should be, I am.'

'I'm intelligent. Really. Everyone says so. I'm not like the others. As for why I chose medicine, you should know, you of all people.' She was twisting her fingers, her big bright eyes intent.

The girls had gathered around the fan in the living room; they took turns gently offering the back of their necks to the cool breeze, chattering away.

'Empty glass, Sara.' He sent her off, then immediately snapped his fingers and said to me, 'Ciccio, ten minutes by the clock. Then drag me off to sleep. No matter what.'

'Couldn't I sit over there? Just for a moment at least. You understand, sir.'

'Don't you dare move.'

She had returned with three glasses. She too took a sip, cautiously, unable to suppress a grimace.

'You're the most elegant man I know. A milord!' she burst out suddenly. 'I swear, Fausto, there is no one more elegant and fascinating than you.'

'By God!' He gave in with a helpless smile. He raised his glass.

'Oh yes. Toast, toast!' Sara was excited.

From the fan the girls leaned forward watching closely, though they didn't have the nerve to move.

'What shall we toast to?' Sara asked anxiously.

'You choose. I assure you, it's for the best.'

'To nothing. Nada. *Al rien ne va plus*. To this life, daughter of the great Buonadonna whom we know . . .' The besotted, tipsy voice of the lieutenant faded away, lost down there in his corner.

'On the contrary, I'll toast to you. To you and to my hopes.

What do you say?' Sara flushed, lightly touching his knee with her fingertips.

'Amen,' he concluded, draining his glass.

'It's time to go, sir,' I tried.

'Fausto, now I have to tell you. Listen to me. Now . . .' the girl continued, trembling a little. Her voice promptly cracked.

'No, keep quiet. Understand? Shut up. For the love of God.' He twisted his head away abruptly.

Those shining eyes closed a moment, then reappeared even more submissive, tired.

'At least tell me why you came,' she tried in a whisper. 'No one thought you would again. Not even Vincenzo. I knew he phoned you, that you spoke together, but that's different from . . .'

'Poor lieutenant.' He smiled. 'Once upon a time he still laughed. Now he no longer even laughs. Just puffs and snorts.'

'Why did you come? Just like that? For no reason?'

'Stop it, Sara. Your sister, your friends: they'll criticize you. Make fun of you.'

'Who's criticizing? Who? Who's making fun? If you only knew how afraid they are of me. And they should be!' She got angry, her face reddening. 'Go on, please, at least tell me this: why you've come.'

'Not without a reason. Since you're so curious. No: not without a reason. But that's enough now. No more questions, young lady.' He put an end to it by getting up, searching for my arm.

On the phone Candida calmly reassured their mother. They would leave soon, it wasn't even midnight. The ice cream was really a disaster.

A flurry of cheerful greetings went around again.

At a very late hour, from my bed, I heard stifled sobs that drew out into weeping which lasted a long time before growing gradually more quiet and stopping. Then steps moving away from the bathroom in the hallway.

Undoubtedly the lieutenant.

9

'My leave is about to expire, sir. I'll have to go back tomorrow. Tomorrow night at the latest.'

'We have plenty of time,' – he waved his hand, annoyed – 'it's not a problem. And if you get back late, you can blame it on me. Right?'

We were in the now empty dining room of the restaurant, all the other tables cleared, the fierce afternoon sun scorching the street outside the windows.

He had retreated into a hopeless black mood, his occasional maniacal outbursts lacking conviction, that wicked cheerfulness I knew in him gone. The shadow of a beard darkened his cheeks.

At the table the girls had surrounded him with attention to no avail, his glass always full, a scoop of clams left at the bottom of the soup tureen just for him, the shade of an awning arranged just right. Sara and Candida's mother, leaving the cashier's desk, turned to him for an opinion, setting aside her absorbed widow's look for a moment.

He put up with it, thanking her with forced smiles. Beside him Sara spoke very little, she too preoccupied by some concern.

'Just one thing, sir. Will you stay in Naples or come back to Turin with me?'

'Good Lord, Ciccio, so many questions. Can't you be quiet for once?' he objected disconsolately.

It was the idea of a party that perked him up a little.

It had been the lieutenant's idea, and now everyone was making an effort to plan it, to make it perfect, just the event that was needed, from the prosciutto to the dessert, from the fish in aspic to the seafood and champagne.

'Uncorked. In a carafe. That way it improves,' the lieutenant explained.

'Vincenzino, you're a turkey as usual,' was his assessment. 'Since when do you put champagne in a carafe? Ignoramus.'

'A venial sin. I won't say another word.' The other, confused, sought to defend himself.

The girls laughed.

'Sara: cat got your tongue?'

'Sara isn't talking. Can't you see she doesn't want any part of it? She's thinking, my God how she's always thinking.'

'Poor Sara, does nothing but think.'

She endured her friends' laughter and irony with her eyes firmly lowered, her hands hidden under the tablecloth.

Then: 'We'd all better go see to our own chores now,' she said dully. 'Go our separate ways. Otherwise we won't have any desire to see each other and celebrate tonight.'

'Don't you feel all right, baby?' he asked. The words fell into a sudden silence.

'Fine. Why? Don't worry about it.' The girl blushed, surprised.

A pale yellow butterfly appeared and flitted along the table in uneven spurts, its tiny wings frantic. Ines, Michelina and Candida raised their hands in confusion, attempting to catch it.

'Nitwits,' Sara muttered, immediately shrugging her shoulders with indifference.

'A butterfly,' I whispered in his ear.

Sara's eyes quickly studied me a moment.

It escaped Ines's fingers and came to rest right in front of him, the two gossamer wings joined on the tablecloth. Without thinking about it, Sara reached out and caught it easily between her thumb and forefinger.

'See?' She laughed.

'Under here, under here!' Candida cried.

A small glass goblet was overturned and the imprisoned butterfly circled around, its wings stretched out low, its trembling antennae exploring.

'Poor thing.'

'What a gorgeous yellow. Look at those black spots. They look just like velvet.'

'Is it true they only live a few days?'

Listless and hot, the girls watched it, resting on their elbows. Now the butterfly stopped; a slight shudder ran through its wings.

'Girls, girls, where do you think you are? Kindergarten? Is that any way to act? A fine consolation!' the restaurant owner's voice complained from the back.

'Signora, let them have fun,' the lieutenant echoed.

'I like the black ones,' Sara said.

'Black? The ones with a skull on their wings? How cheery,' Ines protested.

'Such a long face you have today.'

'Sara, did somebody give you the evil eye?'

'What difference should it make to you people if I like the black ones,' she retorted.

His right hand moved slowly, feeling along the table until the goblet was within reach.

'Black did you say? Are you sure?' he asked her softly, attempting a smile.

'Yes. Why?'

The gloved left hand crashed down on the glass, shattering it amid frightened shrieks.

'There. Now it's black,' he said then, not pulling away from the shards.

'What's going on. What fell?' The lieutenant roused himself. 'Weren't we planning a party?'

'Two assignments for you, Ciccio. My white suit to the cleaners: have it cleaned and ironed, right away. And the champagne. I don't trust the others. That seltzer they'd try to foist on us,' he said.

'Yes, sir.'

'Ten bottles. It won't be too much. Krug.'

'Krug. Yes, sir.'

'Take your time. We're not going out today.'

'That Sara . . .' I began.

'What about her?' I heard his voice lying in wait.

'Nothing. Coming to Naples I would have expected anything, but not these girls. And Sara. I didn't know.'

'And what was there to know?' he snapped. Then, more wearily, 'Worry about yourself, Ciccio. It's useless to make a mystery out of others. Think about yourself, be a tourist.'

From the window of his room, as I was folding the

wrapped-up suit, I saw them in the wicker chairs on the terrace, he undaunted despite the heat, a cigarette dangling from his lip, the lieutenant limp, as though asleep. The sunshade cast a skimpy grey circle, protecting them against the intensity of the sun; beyond the parapet the city's muffled roar extended as far as the deep blue sea.

'Should we talk about it again? Are you thinking about it?'

'No, captain, why? Don't you believe me?' the lieutenant said weakly, his hands trembling at once. 'Didn't we say that discussing it further is worse?'

'Worse, all right.'

'So then, drop it. It's all clear now. Please,' the other breathed, 'we've said everything over and over. Enough.'

'Ten days ago, when I phoned you, and even before, you seemed more certain.'

I stopped fussing with the paper wrapping so they wouldn't hear the rustling. His voice did not seem to have shaken off the sadness that had gripped him in these past few hours.

'But I am certain. Just like you. More than you, maybe, if I may say so. Don't be doubtful, Fausto. Now let's stop it. With this heat . . .' the lieutenant said.

'I heard you. Last night.'

'You shouldn't have. You shouldn't have!' the other cried, but his fury only lasted a moment, the words quavered in his throat again. 'It's my business. Some people cry, some people laugh. What does it matter? What difference does it make? Do you have to teach me everything now?'

'Right. But then, I don't give a damn.'

'If only there were something, just one thing, you gave a damn about,' the lieutenant mourned.

'The way I came into the world, I can go back: alone.

Tomorrow. Tonight. To each his own destiny,' he said brusquely.

'No, no. By now it's all decided. No more misgivings. If you still doubt me now, then you'll offend me. For certain,' the other objected with the faint voice remaining to him. 'But look: it was you who brought it up again this time. You have to admit it.'

'You're right. Touché.' He laughed bitterly.

'And the party? Won't it be a mistake? Those girls, poor things, may the Lord Almighty forever protect them, that Sara who just can't resign herself. And yet she is so intelligent.'

'The party is fine. A great idea. Nothing better. And let's try to enjoy ourselves too.'

'Of course. Such wonderful girls, aren't they? Wasting their time, all that patience, on people like us. Remember Sara and Candida's father? The things he wouldn't do for you. The devotion he showed you. And he probably saw you no more than three times. But you, with Sara, couldn't you . . .'

'Don't even mention her, by God, you big idiot!' he burst out furiously.

I appeared at the door of the restaurant to ask about a nearby dry cleaner. At a table in the dimly lit dining room Sara had her back turned, poring over her books.

'I'm not studying so far in advance, I'm not that fanatical!' She laughed, blushing. 'Just a preliminary glance. The new textbooks. Medicine. How scary.'

'Cheer up. University is the simplest thing. You'll see,' I replied, and told her about the suit.

'How come? Where's the other soldier? That Miccichè, the records clerk? That lazy shirker. He has a special gift for sniffing out the least bit of additional bother. Give it to me. I'll send one of the kitchen boys. Sit down.'

She returned, ill at ease, her arms crossed, hands tucked under her armpits.

'The other girls are preparing things. In the kitchen I'm not worth a thing. Such a disgrace. I just can't learn; certain things women do just don't appeal to me. I'm hopeless. They, on the other hand – you should see how hard they work and how much they enjoy it. And they're still girls, all a year younger than me.' She sat down, closed the large volume and avoided looking at me. 'Can you stay? Just for a minute. Are you thirsty? Would you like something to drink?'

I waited for her to begin, but she kept her eyes on the spine of the book. Rolled up white napkins were set out in double rows. An air freshener had cleansed the air.

'They didn't go to sleep,' I said finally.

'He never rests, that one.' She smiled quietly, a furrow between her brows.

'Neither does the lieutenant.'

'Oh, poor Vincenzo doesn't count.' She dismissed him with a grimace. 'Haven't you seen how he is, a nothing, a nobody? A good man, a saint, certainly, but what does it take for him to be one?'

'They don't even seem like friends.'

She laughed, a sharp burst, then said harshly, 'Nobody can be his friend.'

'I heard them talking, out on the terrace. I couldn't understand. It sounded like some kind of pact.'

'Fausto couldn't make a pact about anything with anyone.'

She brightened a little. 'By now you know how he is. He's one of a kind. A genius. Don't you think so? Either you love him or you don't.'

'He's also a terror,' I ventured.

She laughed happily.

'He certainly is.' She raised her voice a little. 'A terror, a devil, a scourge from God, call him whatever you want. But the others? Who are they, where are they, where are they going, what do they want? Look around, don't you see? The world? A failure.'

She had untucked a hand and was now flicking her thumb repeatedly against her clenched fingers, the nail flat and pink. 'A failure, nothing more,' she repeated slowly.

'I've seen him say and do certain things,' I burst out. 'The arrogance he has! Then of course, a person gives in, justifies it, maybe finds it amusing and even says he's right. I'm his friend for real, and he knows it.'

She shook her head no, that sad mysterious smile of hers back to contradict me.

'Neither you nor anybody else. I've already told you. He's incapable of having any friends. He can't,' she replied.

'Still,' was all I said.

'What I mean is: you may be his friend, I don't doubt it,' she continued, treading carefully on every word, 'but don't you see that you too find yourself arguing with him, objecting, trying to reason with him? And with him there's no reasoning, in his view two and two never equal four, maybe five, maybe three, but never four. You have to take him or leave him.'

'You're a woman and . . .'

'I'm not a woman. If only I were. Or maybe not. What

do I know?' she said morosely. 'What does being a woman or not mean? They say I'm in love with him. Everyone says that, even my mother, poor thing, and behind my back they laugh at me. Only behind my back though. But it's not the foolish kind of love, the fainting and damaging kind that they imagine. I simply decided. I chose. Like a dog chooses to follow someone down the street, and only that someone. He waits. He waits and has no need to explain himself.'

I couldn't meet her eyes, which had become bold as the confession grew.

I felt stupidly disarmed.

'It's not love,' she said. 'It's faithfulness, it's trust, it's believing and waiting. Among other things. Call it, all of you, whatever you want.'

'If you put it that way, there's no use talking about it,' I replied.

'Oh? And why should I bother talking to you?' She reacted violently, taking offence, her big eyes wide. 'You show up, and I was just sitting here waiting to talk to you? At most you can tell me how the trip was, if he coughed a lot, whom he argued with and why. All that.'

'Well. I have to go. The champagne.'

'Please,' she leaned over the table, suddenly limp, 'one more minute. Just one. Don't be angry with me. Tell me about the trip.'

'Tiring. Non-stop. A mad dash. I feel like I've been everywhere and nowhere, I can't explain it. My head is still going round and round.'

'Yes, yes, of course.' She laughed softly and nodded, 'He's possessed, possessed . . .'

'Zoos, high masses, taxis. And you can imagine the insults he tosses around.'

'He doesn't insult, he condemns,' she contradicted with assurance.

'Bars. Drinking. I never saw anyone drink so much.'

'When he drinks he's a god. Don't you think so? Once he said: "Raise those fine flags high . . ."'

'Et cetera, et cetera. I know. It's typical of him when he's dead drunk,' I replied.

'When he's drunk he's magnificent.'

'Maybe because you remember him from your girlhood memories, but—' I started.

'I remember and I know,' she said quickly, 'I know everything. Whereas this world is made up of maggots. In school you study about Olympus, but what's all around you later on? Maggots, which neither speak nor know nor understand.'

Now even her forehead was bent over the book; I saw the tidy, pale parting of her hair, a strand or two lighter at the nape of her neck.

'I'm not an optimist either,' I said. 'Life today is chaos, disaster, we all know it. For us young people . . .'

'I believe in other worlds,' she breathed, her face hidden. 'They say if there were other worlds, they would have tried to communicate with us. Oh, really? What do you think? You, if you were from another world, would you have this desire to communicate? Tell me.'

'I'd have to be crazy!' I laughed.

'Don't you think we're all going to die?' she murmured again. 'Everybody one on top of the other? Is that still living? Life can't go on like this and call itself living. Nobody understands it, but he knows. He knows that we're stupid, trivial, unfit, rotten. He's understood that.'

'May I say something?'

'Go ahead,' she said, resigned.

I paused a moment to line up very carefully the words I needed and set them in the right tone.

'You relate everything to him. You've formed an opinion and you won't budge from it. Fine. But how can that help you? Okay, he's special, very special, no one denies that, but so what? Just because he's blind? There are millions of blind people.'

'We said so before. Vincenzo is also blind. But he's nothing, all air. He doesn't even understand his fate. So he doesn't deserve it.' Stubbornly she shook her small head, which lay in the crook of her elbow.

'What fate? Being blind? It's not like he was born that way,' I suddenly said hotly. 'It's not a Greek tragedy, it's a misfortune. He took it a certain way, given his temperament. It's your fault, your stubbornness, if you want to see it as something else.'

She laughed wearily inside her protective shell.

'Hopeless. You want to probe, explain. You'll never do it. All of you, if you saw an angel standing on a street corner, what would you do? I'll tell you what: you'd count his feathers. To make sure, to verify. That's the way you are.'

She laughed again, but it was almost a sob.

'Try playing this game. Put a blindfold over your eyes, and remain blindfolded in your room or in the park through-out the afternoon. And move around there, explore things, search . . .'

'Is that what you did?'

'Me? What do I have to do with it!' she denied sharply.

'All right. I see. Let's drop it.' I gave in.

'Yes. Drop it.' She seemed to calm down.

'Don't take it so hard.' I pulled myself together. 'I'm not judging you. Nor would I ever make fun of you. Far from it. But maybe you don't understand either. Maybe we're both too young to understand.'

She kept shaking her head in the crook of her elbow, in denial.

'I too know that he's different.' I backed off.

'It's not enough to say he's different. Too easy.' She raised her face, her eyes now a sharp beam aimed elsewhere. 'What about the butterfly this morning? Remember that?'

'Oh. A nice dramatic gesture.'

'A definitive one. I say this to help you understand something.' She scoffed at me from behind that wall of hers. 'Only he is capable of definitive gestures. He thinks of them, he does them. Whoever he catches, he catches.'

'What amazes me is that everybody lets him get away with it. We let him have his way in everything, all the time. Never an objection.'

'He knows,' she continued, her eyes half closed, 'the world is destruction. And he carries this destruction inside him. You see him there, motionless, handsome, but instead, inside, he's filled with devastation. While still showing regard for everything, because he's courteous as well, and when he's angelic no one can equal him.'

'We can go on talking like this for hours. You on one side, me on the other, without reaching any conclusion.'

She agreed with a nod, her gaze bleak, a vein in her neck throbbing rhythmically under the skin.

'And women?' she blurted out suddenly. 'You have no reason to lie to me now. Tell me: did he look for other women during the trip? In Rome?'

'No.'

She took a breath, consoled but sombre.

Then, in a fit of contempt: 'Idiotic fools,' she said. 'They should be chasing after him by the thousands, if they had anything in those heads of theirs. If I were a real woman, the things I'd be able to come up with. For him, incredible things.'

'He's twenty years older than you.'

She laughed. 'Twenty-one. But what am I saying? Ten thousand. A million. And that too is lovely, it's just fine.'

'So then: it's right?'

'Right!' she cried, elated.

She quickly leafed through the book, then handed me a small photograph protected by a transparent sleeve.

She blushed happily. 'Look.'

In her schoolgirl's white knee socks, she barely came up to his waist. They were walking into the sun, his right hand on her delicate shoulder, the bamboo cane nearly obliterated by its own motion. The child was laughing, her teeth gleaming. He, dazzling in white, with the dark splotches of his glasses, his tie, his gloved left hand, cancelled out the few other elements in the picture: a bench, a drab bush.

'From many years ago,' she explained tenderly, her voice a whisper. 'It was my father who took it. But don't tell him. He knows nothing about it. He must never know.'

I suddenly felt discouraged and bewildered in that stifling dimness, with the sharp sting of the air freshener. The words slipped out only because of some obscure rage: 'Tell me, have you ever seen him without his dark glasses?'

The smile that appeared on her face was recognizable as a challenge.

'Of course. Did you think I hadn't, maybe?' she retorted disdainfully. 'But you asked rudely. What were you hoping to do? Scare me? You could never.'

I kept silent, feeling rebuffed, without purpose. That obstinacy of hers had cleared my brain of any intention of being rational, leaving me even emptier.

We stood up. She walked me to the door; from the street came a wall of heat. Loud cries and noises held us there in the doorway.

'A hundred yards, the first one on your right. A posh wine shop,' she explained. 'You can mention the restaurant's name; I've already phoned. Surprised? Why? I have a good imagination, you know. When it comes to him, I can imagine just about anything. I'll bet he wants at least eight bottles.'

'Ten.'

'You see? A gentleman besides.' In the light of day she appeared very pale, the furrow between her brows delicate and deep-set like a dimple. 'Maybe we might have a chance to talk a little more, the two of us.'

'I'm leaving tomorrow night. Or at least I think so. I don't know about him. He wouldn't tell me anything, as usual.'

'He's always been that way.'

'I know. I realized that too.'

She clamped her hands under her armpits again, facing the street and its noises with a stern expression. For a moment she seemed anything but young.

'I didn't ask you about Turin. Silly me. Is it really as beautiful as they say? I'd like to go to university there. I'll have to spend a whole year persuading and reconciling my mother to it, I know that, but in the end . . . I have a peculiar way, if I dig in my heels and push myself, I manage to win. Always.'

'You're very smart.'

'Don't call me smart,' she protested curtly. Her hand waved off my remark. 'I hate the smart girl everyone compliments. I'm determined. That's all. And not a word about Turin. Swear.'

'I swear.'

'Why didn't he go out for a walk today?'

'He didn't want to.'

'If he doesn't walk, at least a little, he gets irritable. There's still time before supper. When you come back, why don't you suggest it to him? By now he may have changed his mind.'

'If I say something, he'll immediately say no. You can bet on it.'

'True, true!' She laughed, revelling in it, her torso swaying, her neck slightly tipped back. 'That "no" of his. Magnificent! A rifle shot, aimed at everything.'

'But I'll suggest it to him anyway, okay?'

She nodded, her teeth nervously pulling at, worrying her upper lip.

'Just one thing,' I ventured, 'you, for four years . . . Writing to him was out, so did you phone him?'

She immediately withdrew behind a glassy smile.

'No,' she replied, her voice strained, 'not a word. That's enough now: I've already said too much.'

'But he . . .'

'He's at the house, he has to walk, has to eat. That's all. Let's leave things as they are.'

'All right.'

'Why, did he say anything to you maybe? About me?' Her voice came out laboured, almost stifled.

'No. Really . . .'

'Not even a word, naturally.' She made a face. 'Now you should go. Take a nice walk, have a look at Naples: it's still a noble city. And be happy.'

'The tourist obeys.' I tried to laugh.

'Just one last thing,' she ventured, overcoming her hesitation. 'I have to trust you. I have no choice. So listen: tonight try not to stick to him constantly like a shadow. Please.'

I felt myself blush. 'It was him. He wouldn't let me move yesterday. I swear I . . .'

She nodded her head, her cheekbones reddened too.

'I know, I know. You don't have to explain. You're not spiteful, I realize that. But tonight, as soon as you can, leave. Don't say a word, just disappear on tiptoe. You too must have needs, every once in a while. Then, too, the house is big. Or you can cosy up to Ines. She's a nice girl, she seems like a silly mischief-maker but she's on the ball, modern. And she looks at you in a certain way. You must have noticed, right? Or doesn't she interest you at all? Just one minute after all. All I need is one minute out of the entire evening. Okay? Tell me you'll do it?'

'I promise. But there's no need for Ines. I mean, don't drag her into it just for that. I can manage.'

She smiled, looking the other way, then hugged herself as if she were cold.

'You feel you are his friend,' she continued, worn-out though by the expenditure of so many words, 'so don't think that in that very minute, this very night, I plan to upset him with anything I say. I wouldn't do that.'

'All right. Then too it shouldn't matter to me. Leave me out of it,' I objected, confused.

'We're all out of it, excluded by him. Some more, some less,' she responded gravely. 'Me like all the others, maybe more so than the others, who knows. But I won't say anything that might upset him. You don't have to worry.'

'Okay, okay. It has nothing to do with me.'

We stood looking at each other a moment longer, embarrassment growing between us.

'Oh I apologize!' She gave a shriek of laughter. 'How rude of me! I didn't even ask you your name. What's your real name?'

I told her my name, albeit reluctantly, by now almost annoyed.

She quickly held out her hand and shook mine eagerly, but immediately pulled free.

'And now I'm going in to face the angry protests of those three flour-coated goody-goodies in there.' She laughed again. 'Women in the kitchen, you have no idea. They all think they're Joan of Arc. Either Joan or Madam Curie.'

She pushed the glass door closed as she stepped back. It shut gently, without a sound, and as it did the pane reflected the frenzied street scene in bizarre overlapping perspectives.

IO

'Vincenzo, Vincenzino, what's come over you? Where are you? Did you have to disappear just now? How can we play if you've disappeared?' the girls cried.

But the lieutenant had dragged himself over to an armchair in the next room, done in by too much food and drink.

'Leave him alone,' he said.

He moved his index finger towards the fanned out, upturned hands, began touching a palm.

'No tickling!' Michelina shrieked, shaking her hand and holding it out again.

'Be still. Quiet, imbecile,' the others protested, excited and very intent.

The finger explored cautiously, lightly.

'A charming mount of Venus: you'll reduce men to ashes,' he pronounced gravely.

'Me, me!' the others were already urging.

'One more thing, please, the heartline,' Michelina pleaded, focused on her palm, on the finger exploring it.

Sara looked at me, she too with her hand outstretched, and a submissive smile that made her seem more tired. I withdrew to the table to station myself in the cross breeze from the two fans. The heat pressed down like a second skin:

not a breath of fresh air from the terrace. Even the fans blew sultry currents of air.

Minuscule residues of ice still floated in a soup tureen. Plates, bowls, cutlery, glasses were piled up in great disarray, covering every last inch of space; a measure or two of champagne, now lukewarm, stood in the bottom of the remaining bottles.

The game continued amid the girls' dazed, edgy laughter. They sat in a circle on the couch, while he, drunk, elbows propped up, indulged in the role of judge.

'The heart line, mine too.'

'And this double M, can you feel it? What does the double M mean?' The breathing of the lieutenant in the other room lay heavily in the pauses, like a death-rattle.

Earlier there had been a song contest while still at the table, after some moribund attempts to make a toast.

'But not a whole song. God help us. Just a stanza. Something humorous. And if you don't know one, forever hold your peace,' he had decreed.

Ines had quickly stood up reciting: 'Peter Piper picked a peck of pickled peppers, A peck of pickled peppers Peter Piper picked.'

'That doesn't count. It's a tongue twister, not a song.' Candida and Michelina spitefully rejected it.

'Who will win the chocolate medal?' he continued, his fork playing a tune on the plates and glasses. 'Come on, Ciccio, let's hear you for once.'

Certain of the effect, with my head buzzing, I belted out:

> *Red is the ass of the ape,*
> *red are the flasks of wine,*
> *red is that sorry ass*
> *of the late Joseph Stalin . . .*

Through the howls of laughter the lieutenant's husky voice could be heard from the head of the table. 'You may be witty, but let's not sink to indecencies . . .'

'Keep quiet, Vincenzino, be good, is it or is it not a party?' the girls retorted.

'Don Vincenzo, don scamorza the wimp,' he scolded him rudely.

But no one could come up with anything more. Eyes bright, they tried to recapture buried shreds of memories, traces that quickly faded on their lips. And a vague awkwardness, distress, in the air.

'Well then,' he said impatiently.

'It's Sara's turn, Sara's turn.'

'Sara, sing? Dream on. She wouldn't deign to.'

'Sara's not here. Don't you see she's not here?'

'You're right. I'm not here. Don't bother me.' She dismissed the girl with a cross look.

Finally it was he who sang, unexpectedly, in a tremulous, gradually more fluid voice, almost moved by the slow measured pace of the stanza, as we listened in a daze:

> *It would be better had I not loved you*
> *I knew the Creed and now I've forgotten it.*
> *And without knowing the Ave Maria*
> *how will I be able to save my soul . . .*

'Oh, Fausto,' the words escaped from Sara's lips.

'And this is your idea of humour?' was the lieutenant's reaction.

'You're right,' he conceded, strangely downcast, his hand already searching for the glass. 'Next. One of you now. Quick.'

'Some party. What fun. A celebration of the Day of the Dead,' the lieutenant, annoyed, went on complaining, using it as an excuse to get up from the table.

Sara had been quick to knock over a bottle and distract her sister and her friends, who were quickly urged to wipe up and clear away.

'I don't love him. Why don't I love him tonight? Dear God, I can't stand him,' she murmured in a corner of the terrace.

She wrung the fingers of her left hand in her other fist, her glistening eyes ringed with dark circles. She tried to take a deep breath but broke off midway, as if suffocating, and ended up twisting her mouth into a grimace.

'Can you understand? Do you see?'

'I think so,' I answered, mentally resigned.

'I'd like to see him dead. Gone. I wish he no longer existed. I can't stand it any more. What do you think? That I'm made of stone? Someone who has no feelings?'

She knotted and twisted the poor little chain around her neck.

'If you want, I'll speak to him. I can try,' I said patiently.

She refused, shaking her head.

'And those three idiots. Listen to them. Three birdbrains. They think they're at the circus,' she protested more wearily.

'It's late already,' I said.

'We'll be here till daybreak. I assure you we'll be here

till morning,' she replied with cold, stubborn anger. 'I'd like to see them all annihilated. Like animals. Smashed, that's what they are. Unfeeling drunks. Never would they recognize someone else's sacrifice.' The words spewed out like bullets.

'Don't overdo it. We know how it is, Sara. All he'd have to do is lift a finger . . .'

Her chin trembled, her shoulders dropped.

'Lift a finger. Right,' she replied stiffly. 'I'd run. Am I or am I not a faithful dog? I'd have to run. But that's all it means. The chill he managed to instil in me tonight! And I'll tell you this: if I were wise, I'd thank him. For the help.'

I leaned on the railing to gaze at the silent city rolled out in lights, and the infinite inky stain of the sea. High above, a constellation glimmered faintly, lost in the mists; a short time earlier the muffled roar of a plane had faded in a drawn-out rise and fall.

'It's my fault, mine alone. It's this defective head of mine. I should chop it off, toss it in the trash,' she went on protesting, a bitter, more ironic tone in her voice, 'incurable fool that I am.'

'It's always our own fault.' I played along to keep her company. 'We're the ones who fabricate, add lustre to other people.'

'You're right.' She breathed out, attempting a smile. 'Him too, poor thing. What should he do? Give me a well-aimed kick, so I'll get it once and for all? It's here, here's where there's a screw loose.' She twirled a finger at her temple.

Then: 'If only my father were still alive, at least. He'd be able to understand. And your father? Is he living? Do you think about him?'

'He is. But I never think about him. I don't know why.' I hardly knew how to answer her.

My mouth felt as though it were on fire from the sauces and the wine, but my brain still reacted lucidly to every stimulus: words, objects standing out vividly in the light, the corner of the piano, the girls' knees as they sat on the couch.

'Now look at them!' she exclaimed. 'They're obscene. Not because of what they're doing, but because of the slightest thing that drives them. Hollow reeds, empty heads.'

In the harsh light of the living room his right hand felt around, encircling and measuring, one after the other, the three ankles lined up in a row. The girls were laughing, first wiggling their feet, then bracing them. They had lost their spontaneity; a sudden awkwardness made their movements more confused and apprehensive.

'A real woman is lord and master of her ankles,' he pronounced, swaying precariously.

'Do you hear him? Did you hear that? The rubbish that comes out of him. I could kill him,' Sara whispered in the darkness, listening intently.

Michelina and Ines had crossed legs to fool him, holding their skirts tight around their knees in bursts of modesty. His thumb and forefinger formed a ring, measured, then uncertain, went back to check.

'Guess, guess!' the shrieks implored.

He knelt down as if sliding off the chair, and carefully fingered them, his thin back curved and his breath laboured.

In the end he gave up with a bored gesture and sat down again, no longer laughing.

'Now I'm going back in and I'm going to slap them. All

of them. First them, then him. A backhander like you've never seen,' Sara said.

But she had already turned around, her elbows on the railing. A childlike yawn crumpled her face.

'Sleepy?'

'Ready to drop,' she sighed, 'but I'm not leaving. Not even if I fall dead asleep. Here I am and here I stay.'

'You'll see: in a minute he'll be the one to come looking for you.'

'I hope he doesn't!' She tried to laugh.

'I'm going to look in at the lieutenant.'

'He's asleep. He's always sleeping, that one. Overwhelmed by his own stomach,' she replied wearily. 'Come back soon, will you? Don't you too leave me here stranded.'

Later on I found him in the bathroom. He was leaning on the edge of the tub, the water roaring out of the tap.

'Is it Ciccio? Good thing. Sit down. Listen how nice it sounds. Water, water,' he faltered, muddled, behind his spent cigarette. 'Stay here. Let's talk man to man.'

'Yes, sir.'

'Confusion. Chaos. Don't you feel like your head too is full of ninepins?'

'It's late, sir.'

'Always late. Never late. Late for what?' He laughed weakly, flinching. He had lost all tension, his thin body swimming like a straw inside his jacket, his shirt rumpled. The rigid glove on his left hand no longer obeyed him, swaying as if it were unscrewed.

With a struggle he pried out his watch, handing it to me.

'Here. A gift.'

'Why, sir? I can't.'

'Don't be a fool. Take it and put it in your pocket. Always. It's the only rule.'

'No, sir. Thank you, but no.' I refused more firmly.

'Because it's gold or just because it's special, for blind people?' He laughed again, turning it in the palm of his hand.

'You promised me a wallet. That's fine. I'd be happy to have it to remember you by. But not the watch,' I said.

He stuck out his lips, already bored. A purplish shadow hollowed out his cheeks; above his collar the folds of skin were pallid and sweaty.

He slipped out his wallet.

'Here. Is that okay?'

I gave up arguing. I emptied the money and documents from each compartment, put them back in the inside pocket of his jacket. He put up with it with no reaction, his shoulders slack.

'That girl—' I began.

'Who? What?'

'Sara. In there. She deserves at least a word.' I spoke loud enough to be heard above the noise of the water.

'Sure. Of course. Why not?' he nodded, swaying. 'And then we'll call the Baron. My poor Baron. All alone up north. You call too. No excuses.'

'Of course, sir. But right now . . .'

'I'm going, you matchmaker. I'm going. I can never say no to anything. "Matchmaker" isn't as offensive as "pimp". That's why I didn't say pimp. See, I didn't call you that. Right?' he laughed, his teeth parting a little. The cigarette fell. He picked it up, held it passively between fingers that seemed unable to grip.

'Never keep the girls waiting. Divine creatures. Always knew it. A man knows.'

'I wasn't talking about the girls. Just Sara,' I said firmly.

'Sara. Right,' he repeated reluctantly, wrinkling his nose.

'Things are quieter now, the lieutenant is asleep, if you go and sit out on the terrace, Sara . . .'

'Don't bury me with words. For God's sake.'

'I'm sorry, sir.'

'I'm going. You keep quiet. Everyone, quiet. And don't turn this off. Leave me this water.'

He got to his feet, overcoming the tremor of his muscles, straightening out his neck and shoulders.

'I'm a dead man, Ciccio.'

'Sir . . .'

'A dead man. What do you know about it? Shut up. A raving dead man.' Rigidly he dragged one foot after the other in the hallway, his right hand stretched out in front of him. 'A drunken dead man. Drunk and disorderly. Is the lieutenant asleep? That stuffed scarecrow. In a quarter, half an hour: everyone out of here. Got it?'

'I'll take the girls home. Don't worry about it,' I assured him.

He laughed shrilly. 'Worry? Why should I worry?'

His right hand groped along the wall.

She was sitting opposite him, arms folded, listening to him talk as he sprawled in a wicker armchair.

Ines was leafing through an old magazine, Michelina and Candida, sulking, went back and forth with piles of dishes, trays overflowing with glasses.

Every now and then the heat of the night seemed to give way to a shiver of damp freshness.

The bright promising jumble of the disorderly room spread out before me as a place that constantly avoids the world's order. Already it was rushing to hole up in some corner of my memory.

Is this all there is to life? I wondered, but dreamily, with no real curiosity.

Ines removed her glasses to give me an uncertain smile. I shrugged with curt, deliberate shyness, and did not move. Fatigue pricked at me here and there, but my head was still alert, eager.

Sara sat through it, frozen, her profile a spot barely visible in the darkness of the terrace. He went on talking, his left hand tucked into his jacket, his right hand slowly waving his cigarette.

Nonsense, naturally. Because every so often I saw Sara, pained, cover her eyes with her hand, as if to shield herself; then she took a breath to draw strength, no longer having the heart to interrupt him, counter his arguments.

He went on and on. His dark head, in stark contrast to the white suit, was thrown back against the backrest of the chair as he uttered all sorts of incoherent insults.

I felt a great temptation to move closer, to overhear a few words.

Sara, doubled over, was trying not to cry, bewildered by that endless stream of words, the faint laughter, that rained down on her, leaving her no way out. She faced him squarely, weakly arching her back, and still he gave her no respite, his teeth and glasses glinting at the slightest move of his head.

Ines stood up, came towards me languidly, her myopic eyes reddened. When she reached the piano, she too turned around to look at them, critical as she took their measure out there, the two of them so different.

'Two actors. Old school, what's more. Out of fashion,' she then remarked softly but firmly. 'Know what I mean?'

'You're wrong,' was my only response.

She stared at me in disappointment, her glasses hidden in her hands. 'Don't tell me you too really take them seriously? I would have thought you were more savvy,' she mocked listlessly.

'At least I respect them,' I said.

She made a nervous gesture, still pondering them through the glass door.

'Respect, hah! They don't impress me one way or the other,' she said firmly. 'What kind of shining example are they supposed to be?'

'An example, I don't know. But they seem exceptional.'

'Time to go,' she concluded, annoyed. 'Sound the muster, soldier.'

Downstairs in the courtyard I finally managed to slow down beside Sara. The others walked ahead more swiftly, legs dancing a jig.

'I don't want to pester you, but if you want to tell me,' I began. 'Was he his usual self? Diabolical?'

She shook her bent head no, biting her lip, intent on studying the courtyard's cobblestones, which formed broad black and white stripes.

'If you want I'll be quiet. Easy to do,' I tried again. 'But it's a mistake.'

'Hopeless. You wouldn't understand. No one would understand,' she replied, though not harshly.

Then suddenly raising her voice in exasperation, 'Where on earth are you all running to? Let's enjoy this breath of air.'

The girls, already at the door, stopped uncertainly; she crossed the courtyard and sat on the step of a dark, narrow staircase that led up into the maze of walls. The smell of damp grass was all around us.

Slowly the girls came back, holding hands, unhappily stifling yawns.

'Sit down,' Sara ordered irritably.

They obeyed after spreading out their handkerchiefs, no longer in good spirits, their heads now nodding.

'A swim would be good, a dip,' Candida's faint voice sighed softly. 'A nice drive and then a swim. Let's go.'

'Why don't you get the car, Sara?' Ines said.

'Dear God, if Mother hears us, at this hour! She'll stab each and every one of us.' Candida laughed. She was resting her temple on her friend's shoulder; the two faces close together stood out like a single bright spot.

'That Vincenzino. What a dud! I'm really sick and tired of him now,' Michelina said.

'He does that every time. Eats and then goes to sleep. Some company. What are we? Nurses? Octogenarians in a home?' Ines added.

'Decent, a good man, that's all they say about him. But who cares about these good men? Are we supposed to become nuns, maybe? And then too, how should he be? Bad?' Michelina complained.

'Still, the party was fun.'

'Thanks to Fausto. Only because of him.'

'The things he comes up with.'

'Fausto is insane. No doubt about it.'

Sara was looking up to where the pinkish glow of lights rose beyond the terrace.

'You're better off giving him up,' Ines tried to tell her.

'I know,' was her calm reply.

'What? Who would have guessed? It's the end of the world.' Ines laughed, surprised. 'Sara and her great love, her passion . . .'

'Don't make fun of her. You make fun of her, then she takes it out on me all day. Leave her alone,' Candida protested, her eyes closed.

'And you, don't you know any funny stories?' Michelina asked, not looking at me. 'You don't talk much. How come? Or is it that we talk too much? Your girlfriends in Turin must be talkers too. Listen: do you know the joke about the transplant? Two friends meet after many years . . .'

'No,' Sara cut her off sharply. 'Shut up.'

'Oh Sara. Stop it.'

'Shut up, I'm telling you. That's nothing but bawdy filth. It's not appropriate,' she scolded.

'It's not appropriate,' the others mocked.

'Did you really say you were giving him up?' Ines went on in another tone, curious.

'I said it. You heard it, didn't you? So then I really said it,' Sara replied coldly.

'Did he treat you badly? Did he insult you?'

'What did he say to you?'

'Was it malicious? But he had been drinking and you . . .'

'That's enough. What does it have to do with you? Mind your own business, if you have any,' Sara retorted harshly.

A faint breath of air began to drift down slowly from

above. The square of sky between the rooftops still looked dark.

They shifted their shirt collars to feel the cool freshness, a few hands fanned the air to blow more life into the modest breeze.

'Sara G. wouldn't have had a good ring to it. I can't picture it,' Michelina sighed.

'The surname test again, as usual. Kindergarten children, that's all you are,' Ines snapped.

'You. What's your last name?' Candida asked.

I told them, lowering my voice for some reason, whereas when they talked they trumpeted every word.

They began pairing up my last name with their first names, one after the other, interrogatively or affirmatively, laughing, intoning each syllable, first quickly then stressing them, the better to judge the combination, the sound.

'The only one it goes well with is Ines!' Candida finally laughed.

'The surnames of the north: curious, even appealing, but harsh, they have no music,' Michelina pronounced.

'Silly fools. You're nothing but three pathetic fools,' Sara assailed them in a sudden outburst. 'Ineffectual birdbrains. Why must I always have you around me?'

'Oh sure, your brain is rational, falling for that unfortunate loser,' Ines rejoined angrily.

The agreeable affability on the steps unravelled in a rowdy brawl.

'Either you keep that malicious mouth of yours shut or I'll—' Sara threatened, already on her feet.

'Or you'll what? Go ahead. Tell me. Say it. Just try it, I'd like to see you!' the other girl shrieked.

Candida and Michelina were watching me, waiting for me to intervene. But it was Sara who got sidetracked.

'Why did that light up there go out?' She remained rapt, staring towards the terrace.

We all turned, the greyness of the distant windows just visible at the top of the wall.

'Why did he need to turn off the lights? Why would he?' Sara asked again, peering up.

I didn't have time to say a word.

The first gunshot, though from a closed room high among the walls, came roaring down on us, the sound already shattered in endless reverberations.

I was racing up the stairs when the second shot, more muffled, exploded.

And as the shrieks and screams of the fleeing girls faded behind the door, as I heard Sara breathing hard behind me, I had a momentary clear awareness that all of it – those shots, my sprint, the darkness and the hour and him up there – could not possibly have ended otherwise.

But when we reached the landing my hands were fumbling, and it was Sara who angrily snatched the keys from me.

She moaned, her mouth tight, trying the door.

'I should have known, I knew it, I always knew it, silly fool that I am,' I thought I heard her say.

The pitch darkness in the hall stopped us.

'Quick!' Sara cried.

Shutters banged inside the courtyard, and there was even a voice, I thought, but it immediately fell silent.

In the room next to the living room the lieutenant was slouched in his armchair, his head sideways, a thin trickle of blood from under his ear dripping into his collar. And him, a few steps away: standing there, his arms dangling, his lips twisted and crumpled.

The gun: black on the carpet, in the few inches between the armchair and his shoes.

I couldn't make myself go in, my shoulders and knees suddenly leaden. I saw Sara approach him, trembling, she grabbed one arm then the other with increasing force and desperation, to drag him, pry him away.

'Do something! You! Something!' she shrieked.

I couldn't answer her, my breath frozen between my teeth. It wasn't fear, not at all, but rather an insurmountable, boundless inertia that sandbagged my veins and my sense of reality, and made me insensible to that place, to any possible pain.

Vincenzo V.'s bulk between the two arms of the chair seemed swollen, a gelatinous grey and white heap.

And she was still tugging. She pushed him as far as the doorway where he stood leaning against the door jamb, rigid, bent over like a marionette, barely breathing.

'You and your God! Why don't you move?' Sara cried again, widening her eyes at me.

'No. It's not true. No . . .' his wooden mouth uttered confusedly.

But Sara had already managed to place a glass in his right hand, and with mechanical obedience he brought it to his lips, drained it. It might seem that the violent impact of his cough would be able to stir him, rouse him, but instead his fingers quickly let go and the empty glass dropped.

'His belongings. Quick!' Sara yelled, holding him up against the wall with both hands.

I ran here and there without thinking and returned with an armful of clothes, my uniform, medicine bottles inside the jumble in his military bag, the bamboo cane. Desperate, I kept trying to search my brain for all the things I had missed and left scattered between the two rooms and the bathroom.

'Idiot, the suitcase!' Sara ordered in an icy voice, yanking a vial from the satchel.

From the hallway, as I mindlessly stuffed the suitcase, I saw her open his mouth, cram in a sleeping pill with steady fingers, make him drink again.

With her arms around him, she tried to drag him to the door.

'Quick,' she urged, pressed against him.

'What about him? How can we— Where are you thinking of going? It's the stupidest thing,' finally came from my throat.

'That one must already be dead,' she cried straining. 'And what does that have to do with us? You don't want to? Do as you like.'

Inwardly I was swearing up a storm as I bent over the suitcase: I'm not leaving here, let them go, as soon as they run off I'll call someone, or else I'll phone; then tonight, my train.

I heard her groaning from the landing.

I carried the suitcase out. She looked at me pathetically; he was in total collapse between the wall and that embrace.

'Down to the door. Just as far as the door. Show some mercy. Help me. Then I'll get the car. And you won't have to give it another thought, you won't be involved any more,' she sobbed.

We dragged him down the stairs. He was light and disjointed, like a bundle of dry twigs. In the courtyard she was quick to check the balconies and shutters upstairs and down, but everything seemed bolted up, deserted.

I opened the door, leaned him against it.

'Just for a minute. Not even a minute—' She ran off, angrily wiping away tears from her eyes.

'Sir,' I tried, 'can you hear me?'

I was holding him up with my hand under his arm braced against the rough wooden door.

His head lolled as though unhinged, from his nostrils came harsh, laboured breathing.

The three girls suddenly flashed into my mind. Who knows where they'd run off to? By this time they must already have awakened mothers, fathers, relatives and told them everything. And the people facing the courtyard, those slammed shutters, that voice . . .

I heard the car screech.

'In back. Here, in back. Careful. Slowly,' Sara whispered, moving the seats forward to make room.

I saw a bottle of whisky on the seat, a blanket.

He lay curled up there in the back like a poor ungainly dog, ridiculously pale. His dark glasses slipped but Sara's hand stopped them. Carefully and gently she put them back in place.

'Go now. Dear God, go, don't give it another thought,' she said, sitting behind the wheel.

'But where? And you? Where are you running to now?'

'I know a place,' she replied without looking at me, the engine running, her white knobbly fingers tightly gripping the steering wheel.

The road, empty and clear, stretched ahead in sharp curves, still dark, though the headlights were already paling against the effect of the brightening sky.

'You're making a big mistake. It's pointless to run away. It's worse that way. Don't you see?' I tried to reason with her.

The image of the lieutenant in the armchair, that red trickle behind his ear, flashed before my eyes.

'Will you go?' she screamed, though quickly controlling her voice. 'Who asked you for anything? Go away. Beat it. It's my business, our business.'

I opened the car door again.

'I brought him here. I'm responsible,' I objected fiercely. 'Dead drunk as he is, you made him swallow a sleeping pill to boot. He could drop dead here, right now, do you realize that?'

She nodded weakly, but as though what she heard was of no importance. Her chin was trembling, but she had managed to contain her tears.

'Whatever may have happened,' she said then, 'let's take him someplace, away from here. So he can wake up there, explain it to us. Have time to think straight. As soon as he wakes up, he'll decide. He'll be the one to decide. We can do that, that much at least. For him.'

Her voice died in her throat.

'But where will you take him?'

'Don't worry about it,' she retorted, then quickly, reluctantly added: 'To a house my mother owns. Not far away. It's empty, there's no one living there. Come on. Before he wakes up.'

'Why? I don't get it. Why do you want to do this? We're the two most foolish . . .'

I couldn't think of anything else to say.

'My darling, my poor angel. I should have known, I should have . . .' she murmured, staring at the road.

Legs, shoulders, arms were already moving independently of the lifeless, arid void I felt inside.

I was aware of sitting down, closing the door.

The car jerked forward.

Lying dishevelled behind us, he was coughing, his mouth open. When the coughing stopped, his breathing was laboured.

'Mother of God, will you loosen that damned tie of his? Let him breathe at least!' she barked.

'It's the sleeping pill you stuck in him. The drinking. He's in bad shape. We should—'.

'Nothing. We should do absolutely nothing,' she snapped.

She was driving in angry jolts, her face tense and clenched like a fist. The dark rings under her eyes had devoured half her cheeks. She was peering into the rearview mirror, relying only on her hands to follow the road. At a crossroads we skidded fearfully on a rail junction, miraculously avoiding a tram platform.

'Two more minutes and we're there,' she said.

'And then? What do we do then?'

'We're just there,' she shouted, tears suddenly appearing. 'The important thing is to get there. Give him time.'

'You're nuts. And I—'

'I don't want to hear it. Shut up, don't tell me!' she shouted again, leaning over and wrenching away from the wheel. 'You? Who cares about you! Who asked you for anything? Who are you? Why didn't you disappear, like you wanted to!'

'Hey, Sara!' I too shouted.

She swallowed, tensing the muscles of her arms and torso to give herself strength and regain control.

'Okay,' she said quietly, 'okay. Tell me.'

'Nothing. Nothing.'

Everything had once again distanced itself from my heart. Unreachable. In my gaze, those fleeing walls, narrow roads, the sky above now indifferent and hostile.

'Talk to me. I'm sorry.'

'Just this: you should be careful. *We* should.' I spoke without conviction, my own voice detached from me. 'But what are we doing? Let's not make matters worse. You think you're helping him. I'm here for the same reason. But what if—'

'Why two shots?' she interrupted, not paying any attention to me. 'Did you notice that? Two shots?'

A sudden apprehension cleared the cobwebs out of my head.

'Maybe the first one missed. Or they shot just to test the gun,' I said.

'Why do you say "they"? Who did? Him. Just him. He shot, tried, maybe missed the other shot. At himself. They had decided together, but he was the only one who shot,' she suggested, her voice cracking.

'Decided? To commit suicide together?'

A moan escaped her.

'You think they made a pact? All planned out?' I asked again.

She nodded, her lips sealed.

'Couldn't it have been the drinking? All the rest too, of course, but especially tonight's drinking . . .'

'No, no,' she objected wearily. 'They were prepared. Now I realize it. Even the party. All an understanding between the two of them. That's why he came. For that reason. And I, damned fool not to have seen it right away, God help me . . .'

'But what about him, then. Why nothing?'

'He must have missed. Or dropped the gun. And we got there too soon,' she suggested with some confusion.

'Or because he was drunk too. His fingers couldn't even hold a cigarette. Or maybe he was afraid.'

'No, it wasn't fear,' she disagreed.

'Why not? At the last minute . . .'

'He wasn't afraid. Not him!' she shouted again.

I didn't have the energy to contradict her. And it all seemed unimportant. I could still hear those gunshots in my head, and picture the lieutenant's body slumped in the armchair, dead or alive. But those images and sounds were insignificant, merely exaggerated, superfluous: they had nothing to do with reality, mine, ours, his as he lay obliterated in sleep.

'We're here. Right behind there,' she announced unemotionally, accelerating.

Only then did I notice the narrow road with its steep curves, between chipped walls and glimpses of dark green: gardens divided by wire fencing.

We turned onto a dirt track and when I got out of the car I saw the edges of several low houses, set apart among the locust trees. The calm, flat surface of the sea, still grey, was far in the distance. It was daybreak: a promising, chalky light preceded the sun, distinguishing the contrasting spaces and forms of the surrounding trees, the minute fiery spots of ripe tomatoes in the gardens, the jumbled rooftops of the darkened city that lay supine down below.

The house was abandoned: not a chair, not a stick of furniture, just rolls of dusty old carpets along the wall of the largest room. Even the inside doors were missing. A faint pale light seeped in from the closed shutters. I could smell the scent of whitewash, of moss-grown wood.

'Over there, in the hallway. What are you waiting for?' she asked, pointing to the carpets.

She settled him near the bathroom door on the rolls, his back against the wall, the blanket covering him from ankles to stomach. With a timid gesture, immediately withdrawn, she brushed his hair at the temples, smoothed his forehead. She turned the taps on in the bathtub and the sink, letting the water run full tilt. She placed the open bottle a few inches from his right hand.

Finally she stood looking at him, her clenched fists clamped under her arms.

'Poor angel, at least some water, no?' I heard her barely whisper. 'And you, good Lord, if you would . . .'

I went outside to sit on the step. An electrical wire without a bulb hung from the doorway, the few feet of dirt in front of the house were invaded by yellowed weeds and scorched scrub.

I saw the looming morning light grow all around in silence. Distant humming already filled the air and a chirping came from far-off trees, but I was too wasted by fatigue to ask myself any more questions.

It wasn't a wall, but a kind of precariously high metal fence, perhaps hundreds and hundreds of headboards, that I had to climb, fearful of falling and splatting. My cement feet would not move, refused to obey me. From up there, swaying, a soldier was shouting something at me, a blank comic-strip balloon with no words came from his uselessly waggling mouth . . .

I woke up.

From my watch I saw that I had slept for less than half an

hour. I shivered despite the fact that the air was already warm. A murky consciousness broke in on me again.

She too was sitting on the step, elbows and forehead resting on her knees.

A cigarette, right. But no matches. With a great deal of caution I moved into the hallway, drew back his blanket, and rummaged for his lighter.

He was breathing more regularly, his brow damp with a film of perspiration.

Strolling around the house I saw only piles of debris, pieces of wood, a bucket with no bottom. The ground quickly rose more steeply among scattered trees with rust-coloured trunks to a structure half-hidden by foliage, branches on which large patched sheets were hung out to dry. A stray yellow dog stared at me from afar, wagging his tail suspiciously. He disappeared, running crookedly beyond the curve of the hill.

'Why do you think we made a mistake?' she greeted me, barely raising her face.

She was exhausted, beaten. But my thoughts too were fragmented, lifeless.

I sat down on the grass, careful, however, not to sit facing those dark circles under her eyes.

'Running just to get away, we should have taken everything with us. Our stuff, the lieutenant,' I strained to reply. 'Do you realize how many things we forgot? Shoes, the gun, the other suitcase. What's the point of running away like that?'

But each word weighed me down as soon as I said it: a stone plunging into the dark pit of a well, that's what I was.

She didn't answer, her face once again hidden in her arms, her shoulders rising faintly as she breathed.

'Your sister, the other two, by now they must have told the whole story to any number of people,' I continued. 'And let's hope so, given how stupid we were. Let's hope the lieutenant isn't dead, that someone came to his aid. What more can I say?'

'So you're having second thoughts. If you are, what are you still doing here? Did I beg you to stay? Go ahead, go to the lieutenant, go wherever you want,' she replied from inside her shelter. Not angrily, though.

'What does that have to do with anything? Could you stop that? I'm here, aren't I? I'm here, right? So cut it out,' I retorted half-heartedly.

She yawned, jumped down from the step, smoothed out her sleeves, her white blouse all crumpled.

'God, if only I at least had a comb.' She tried to laugh. 'That uncouth habit of mine, going around without a purse. Do you think they'll come looking for us? Way out here?'

'How do I know?'

'How long does it last, that sleeping pill?'

'Not long. Hardly any time. Always just a short while, I think. Depending on how many he takes,' I said.

'Of course. It is addictive. Anyway he'll wake up soon. And be able to decide. You'll see.'

She paced up and down in front of me, two steps towards the car, two steps back towards the house, the weeds crunching under her feet. I watched her walk back and forth rubbing her arms, which had gone to sleep, feeling her face, her hair at the back of her neck.

'If he wanted to die as you say, will he still be capable of deciding anything?' I asked.

She stopped, the tip of her shoe idly jabbing at the dirt.

'I'm not afraid. Not in the least,' she said softly. 'I would go back right now, if it would help him. Could we have left him there? So he could go through a thousand miseries? What else could we have done? For you it's different, I know that.'

'I should be on the train, that's where. My leave has run out. Assuming nothing else happens, at best I'll end up in jail. Satisfied?'

She laughed, pacing again.

'And what would that mean, to a soldier? Inside or out, isn't it all one and the same? Tell me, do you have any money?'

'Why?'

'Before everybody gets out on the streets,' she thought quickly, 'we should buy something. A container of coffee, cigarettes, croissants if you can find them. Will you? There's a shop immediately to the right after the track. They have everything. You'll be gone and back in five minutes.'

'Why me and not you?'

The dusty tip of the shoe quickly lost patience and began jabbing again.

'I won't leave him,' she objected calmly. 'Where he is, that's where I stay. Then too, around here they remember my mother. It's best if they don't see me. Right? But if you don't want to, don't go. I don't want to force you.'

'Right now?' I gave in.

'Try. What can you lose? People get up early here, they're farmers after all. Just think: some nice hot coffee. It would do us all good.'

I stood up, muscles stinging as they stretched beneath my skin.

'A candle too,' she was quick to add, 'it's always better to have one than be caught without.'

★

The old woman kept working the lever of the espresso maker. The drab wrinkled arm pumping away did not prevent her from giving me a half-smile.

'You have to be patient. The water isn't hot yet. Meanwhile look around. You might see something else. We have everything here. Like in the city.'

A curtain closed off the shop in back. The small area was cluttered with boxes and display cases, cans stacked in a pyramid stood on the shelves. A large hand scale was tossed on some baskets of vegetables.

I spotted the telephone over a tower of colourful packages, the directory hanging from a chain.

Candida, I immediately thought. Ines . . . I can't remember her last name. Or else the lieutenant's house. I just need to hear a voice, anyone's, to know how things stand. Of course I'll hang up without a word. Or would this too be a mistake?

My imagination exhausted, for a moment I chased nameless shadows back and forth through those rooms.

'It's still not as it should be. But if you want to try it—' the old woman called me back as she moved down the counter with a cup of coffee.

As I drank it, I felt every fibre languidly drenched by those few drops of warmth.

Newspapers, I thought.

'Newspapers? Those we don't have. Not until later. Around noon, sometimes not even,' the woman apologized with a toothless frown. 'Has something serious happened? More wars? What is this world coming to. Tell me, you know more than I.'

I went out with the package. The bottle of coffee was hot and I had to continually change hands.

Time seemed endless, a boundless space, more barren and blank than the already sunny sky. But elsewhere, in those rooms down there, messy with dishes and glasses, and back in the barracks, and on my northbound train, that same time was instead fleeing, flashing past much too quickly, robbing me, accusing me.

The dirt track was steep. I wondered how Sara had managed to drive it so easily. The car and house reappeared after a sharp curve.

She was still on the step. Seeing me with the package and the coffee, she raised a hand as if to shout 'bravo'.

'He's still asleep,' she said, getting up. 'Should I try to wake him? Would it be better?'

'Let's wait. Another hour. It's early.'

'An hour,' she agreed.

She took the bottle, uncorking it eagerly.

'Not even a glass. What a house and what a worthless so-and-so,' she scolded.

She drank, pressing her chest against the heat.

'Good. It will still be hot when he wakes up. What are those, marzipan? No croissants?'

She seemed anxious to do something again, to keep busy. I looked at her, trying to make her see how exhausted I was. Quickly she shrugged. Her eyes looked away.

'Who do you think will come?' she said softly. 'Carabinieri or the police? Better the carabinieri, don't you think?'

No one will come. I felt it hit me like a thud: no one will look for us, nothing happened, Vincenzo isn't dead, everything is still going on as usual and we will keep wandering senselessly through this parched air, back and forth like flies, like specks of dust.

To break the silence I said, 'Carabinieri. And who would lead them here?'

'My mother. My sister. They're the only ones. Who else could ever imagine?' She sighed.

She tucked her hands into her belt like an awkward boy.

'Exhaustion is a bad counsellor,' she went on. 'Let's not worry about it. Here we are and here we'll wait.'

'Yeah. Right,' I said.

'Right,' she smiled briefly.

'Who knows? Maybe there's still time. Who can say?' I murmured but without conviction.

'Sure. Of course,' she agreed quickly, happy to have a pretext. 'He'll straighten things out. As soon as he wakes up, he'll take care of everything. I can already see him. I swear.'

'He'll straighten things out if the lieutenant is alive. Otherwise what's left to straighten out?' I replied.

'Of course he's alive. Fools never die. Not even after being shot,' she snapped fiercely.

'Sara . . .'

She looked away from me.

'Okay, okay. You're right,' she replied, her voice by then indifferent. 'Even I know that I don't always think clearly, that I make mistakes and make things worse all the time. I know it. If my mother could see me, poor woman. She'd have me walled-up alive. You can't begin to imagine.'

12

A parade of ants, big and shiny, moved along a thin trail of dust that zigzagged through the weeds, their abdomens rippling as their legs jostled forward. The orderly line broke up into feverish whirling at the base of a tree trunk, in the mealy opening of a root.

'Go on. Just for a minute. Please,' she said anxiously. 'I'll start waking him up. Let me do it. Then I'll call you. I'll call you.'

I looked up at the sound of an aeroplane. The triangular grey silhouette appeared sharp and bright against the sky, headed towards the city. It veered off into the distance, already silent, the rumble absorbed by then.

It was eight o'clock. Maybe if I lay down I would be able to sleep a little. But the desire to sleep was both strong and remote. Idle thoughts clogged and plagued my brain, slow to quiet down: whether to put my uniform back on, for example, or remorse at having sent only a single postcard home.

The shapes of my father, my mother, the Sardinian soldier who slept to my right in the barracks, did not contain any real human features; they were merely fixed points, dots indicating a neutral place which had less and less to do with me.

No sign of life from the house. Maybe she hadn't yet been able to wake him, maybe she was just sitting there without rousing him, without calling to him. Mesmerized as usual, of course; as soon as she sets eyes on him she's lost, a sheepish child. So much for her fine decision.

Nothing has happened, no one has actually died, I know it, we're just in a world of our own, cut off for some reason yet still clinging to this last crust of earth by our fingernails, still unaware that before long we'll be back among the others and it will all be as it was before and we'll forget, we will forget. My leave has expired – did it expire last night or this morning? – I'd better put my uniform back on . . .

I lit another cigarette, my mouth like glue. I couldn't taste anything any more, my tongue limp, gritty. A spot had somehow got on my sleeve. With two fingers I picked up an ant, choosing one of the largest ones; as it thrashed its legs and antennae frantically in the air, the parade went on with its bustle, rushing around in the dirt, back and forth to the root.

'To hell with you too,' I said, dropping it among the taller, tangled bushes.

Now I'll get a move on, I'll get up and go over there, I'd better keep an eye on them, not leave them alone.

I took another look around: the edges of the houses among the locust trees, the distant sea flat in the ashen grey mist, the bright green of the trees.

The exhaustion I felt was even pleasurable at times, it cautioned me tenderly from every muscle, making me more aware of various frailties, pangs, tremors.

She appeared in front of the house, her hands over her face.

I ran to her.

'He doesn't want me,' she sobbed without uncovering her face. 'He doesn't want me. He chased me away.'

'But is he all right?'

She nodded behind her hands, a dry sob.

'Did you talk? Does he remember? Does he know where we are?'

She shrugged, stepped back blindly until she felt the step behind her heels. She sank down on it.

It took me a few seconds to tear myself away from there and go inside. My head felt empty, roaring, and though I knew that emptiness was deadly, I fumbled in vain to have a couple of words ready on my tongue, in my brain.

He was still on the carpet rolls, the blanket thrown off, the coffee bottle between his right hand and his stomach. Sara must have wiped his face with a wet handkerchief, I saw the scrap of cloth tossed in the sink.

'It's me,' I said quietly.

I didn't seem to feel emotion or fear or pity, I saw him as a human wreck, an unfamiliar presence in a hospital ward.

'Ciccio,' was all he said.

And his muscles relaxed.

I bent down, lit a cigarette, held it within reach of his lips. He leaned forward eagerly.

'Friend,' he said.

His voice was hoarse, slurred by the sleeping pill. He removed the cigarette to cough, drink a sip of coffee, then cough again in a lengthy release.

A couple of inches, give or take, of a slimy liquid remained at the bottom of the bottle.

'Ciccio,' he repeated.

'Yes, sir. I'm here. Are you all right?'

The cigarette rolled slowly between his lips from one corner to the other then dangled as if he no longer wanted it.

'Who's there? Is someone with you?'

'No one, sir. Just us.'

He tried to smile, grateful, but very weak.

'Ice. Get me some ice. To chew. Right away,' he said faintly.

'There is no ice. Not here,' I told him.

'No?' He roused himself slightly. 'Why not? What's going on. Here? What does "here" mean?'

I started talking, trying to be very brief, gradually lowering my tone as if it were just any ordinary story, unrelated, to be told in the most concise way possible, with the economy of a newspaper ad.

He was leaning his head against the wall. For an instant the cigarette smoke rushed more quickly from his nostrils. When I finished talking he didn't say a word. The cigarette burned down to a stub. I reached out two fingers; he docilely allowed me to remove the butt.

'We have to decide,' I said after a while.

'What? Who's there. Still just you?'

'Yes, sir,' I went on nervously. 'Me and Sara. We waited. For you to wake up. To decide. It's late. Almost nine o'clock.'

'Nine,' he echoed.

The grooves of the two lines between his nose and cheeks had deepened as if drawn with indelible ink. He handed me the coffee bottle, I put the whisky flask in his hand. He held it against his cheek, turning it to capture its coolness, but did not bring it to his lips; he pushed it away, refusing it, his right hand trembling.

'I should call Sara. Say something to her?' I began again. He shook his head, his brow creased.

'She's outside. Crying. She's worn out. Shouldn't we now . . .' I continued.

He reached out his hand, I felt its grip on my arm, but nagging, not strong.

'Give her something to do. Or send her away. If she doesn't go away, make sure she always has something to do. So she doesn't think. So she doesn't hang around me,' he whispered in anxious bursts.

'But sir, we—'

'She mustn't stay here. I don't want her,' he went on desperately, clearing the gluey mucus from his throat. 'I'm the one who should go. Go away, vanish, drop dead. Get it? I failed tonight, God damn me. But now I won't. Now I won't. You're my friend. You still are, right? Help me.'

His fingers went on worrying my arm from wrist to elbow, convulsively.

'Sir, but I—'

'Quiet. For God's sake. Shut up. Don't say a word. I can't disgrace myself. Disgrace myself on top of it all: no,' he finished, a sharp rasping cough lurking behind every word. 'I'm not a lion. I thought I was, but no. I'm not. Poor Vincenzino, the mess I got you into . . .'

Later on I managed to persuade him. I put the bamboo cane between his fingers, helped drag him to his feet to take at least two steps outside.

I felt him trembling very faintly at my side, a papier-mâché puppet, his gait hesitant, clumsy for the first time, his cane having given up exploring.

When he came down the step, he flinched, as if what seemed to affect him wasn't the sun, the light, but the foul breath, the chafing of some unknown beast.

'No,' he barely managed to say.

But he slumped against me, his balance gone.

I dragged him carefully to the shade of a tree. Sara immediately appeared from behind the house. She was biting her knuckles, her eyes frightened, intent on every little move we made, on him as he slowly folded his brittle legs, sat down on the grass. Even there, he showed no interest in feeling the bark of the tree behind him, the bristly ground around him.

Resorting to gestures, spreading my arms, moving my fingers, I tried to explain. But Sara, motionless, wasn't even looking at me, riveted only on him.

When she decided to return my gesturing, she made a disconsolate, meaningless sign, then squatted on her heels, no longer daring to approach.

Incredibly long minutes went by, my eyes bewitched by the dizzying sweep of the second hand on my watch. A solitary cicada suddenly broke the silence, high up behind us.

He was breathing harshly, the grating of each breath of air like screeching on glass.

'No excuse,' he shuddered.

I had to hold him up before he lost his support against the tree; he recovered his position but without being aware of his muscles' movement.

'Feeling better, sir?' I asked softly.

'Oh, it's you. Tell me I'm not here. Vanish: make me feel like I'm not here,' he said through his teeth.

I saw Sara get up, tiptoe cautiously, gently to our tree, a finger to her lips, having overcome any uncertainty.

She sat down next to him.

The gentleness with which she managed to bend his shoulder, soften the remaining tension of his frame until she was able to cradle that head in her lap, made my heart almost painfully skip a beat. His right hand rose a moment to object, but quickly dropped back ineffectually.

'No,' he moaned, 'no.'

'Hush,' Sara silenced him in a soft singsong voice. 'Hush. Don't think any more. Not a thought.'

She smoothed his hair with brief, fearful touches, brushing his forehead as if he were a sick child. Finally, very pale, she encircled his head in her arms.

I moved over on the grass to put some space between us.

'No, not this,' he was still moaning. 'No.'

'Hush,' she whispered, her gaze lost in the distance. 'Hush. Why suffer? No more. Not any more.'

And she rocked him gently.

'Life is draining away. Feel it? Draining away.' His broken words intermingled weakly with Sara's hushes. 'It hurts. But it's right. Right . . . I'm a coward, a—'

'Hush,' she kept saying softly, prevailing over him. 'You mustn't think. You mustn't.'

'I was afraid . . .'

'We're all afraid, all of us. Hush. Rest, my angel,' Sara went on. For a moment her dark eyes strayed to me, quickly passing over me like some annoying obstacle.

I was no longer moved now, just scared, helpless. I went back to the step in front of the house. The sun was already beating down fiercely.

They were a single pale spot, dappled with the gentle brush strokes of the tree's shadow. And I was outside, driven away, overwhelmed by need.

Shortly afterwards I went back in to put on my uniform.

13

I sat on the edge of the tub in the bathroom. The water had run out: little more than a trickle, not even cool, dribbled slowly through my fingers.

My military trousers and shirt hung on me like the shabby clothes of a bum. I couldn't find my tie or my belt. And I seemed to give off the sour, dead odour of spoiled rations.

Okay, so be it. I will not expect anything any more, attempt anything, I won't make a move, I won't think about it any more.

I rinsed my mouth with a shot of whisky; I started examining myself lazily in the tiny mirror over the sink. The dark stubble of my beard made me look even worse, my cheeks were a greasy grey membrane. Mortified, I started rinsing myself, cupping my hands under that trickle of water, one meagre splash at a time, my eyes hurting at the slightest pressure on my eyelids, the refreshing effect of those few drops quickly gone.

Maybe I was hungry too, or nauseous somehow. The bag of marzipan had been left somewhere, not to anyone's taste. As in a very distant, very soft glow, I saw again the table laid the night before, Candida, Michelina, Ines exultant, vying to set out dish after dish, and at each plate his shouting, his laughter, the lieutenant's gluttonous demands.

Ines: who knows how much talking she's done by now.

They were still there, silent, Sara's left hand placidly sweeping the air to interrupt the annoying flight of an insect. He sprawled limply as if asleep.

A cicada was singing. The weeds and grass seemed even more withered in the harsh light, the sky a painful blue. A double white stripe began streaking it swiftly, without any blurring or sounds: a jet plane, almost invisible, at a very high altitude.

Go ahead: unload it. Open your filthy holds and spew out those hundred or hundred thousand megatons that are in your belly. Blow us up and get it over with, there's really nothing left to save. Amen. Why tomorrow, when it's convenient for you? Why not now, right away?

But even this loss in me and of me, which I bore as it simultaneously demolished me and shaped me, was not true conviction; it was not an absolute desire to obliterate and be obliterated, but only a reflection of a lack of raison d'être, of life, which was elusive.

A reason for being, and a life that I could no longer make sense of, one distorted and poisoned by what had happened, the trip and him and his furious whirlwind of words, those two shots that still echoed, the lieutenant bloody in his chair, and now, worst of all, harshest of all, the image of the two of them out there: washed pale like a watercolour in the friendly shade of the tree, immersed, unreachable, enclosed in a serenity that was insult and scorn, even if it was only the paltry serenity of a performance.

Once again I realized that it wasn't fear or even envy, but

a frozen wall that had dropped down to isolate me from everything familiar or possible.

I toyed with the box of matches, and watched them. Amidst the greenery, the foliage, they seemed like a pale vanishing point, more and more uncertain and transparent.

Now they'll vanish and with them the tree, this place, this time, I thought.

It was eleven o'clock.

I closed the window again, folded my clothes after sniffing the mysterious stain on my sleeve to no avail, and rummaged through my suitcase again, all the while knowing I would not find toothpaste or a razor there. They would have consoled me, emerging unexpectedly from that tangle of stuff.

'Ciccio. Come on over. The bottle too,' I heard him call me. They were smoking, sitting shoulder to shoulder. From the way he reached out his right hand for the whisky, I quickly guessed that he was more rested and in control. Sara's eyes were alight with a new passion.

'Sit down. Why did you disappear? Or were you sleeping?' she asked.

She had recovered her normal voice, slower, with barely concealed exhaustion.

'Here I am, sir.'

I squatted in the grass; the sun as it rose higher had reduced the circle of shade around the tree.

He reached out a hand to touch me, feeling the epaulette on my military shirt.

'The stars already,' he remarked. 'We're clearing out, then. Excellent.' I was distracted by Sara.

With a smile that was naive rather than convinced, she

nodded to make me understand: the crisis was over, everything was all right now.

'You're the ones who count, not me. All smoke and no fire, that's me,' he said sadly but without hesitation.

'That's where you're wrong. The best part of the fire is the smoke, its scent,' Sara tried to tell him.

He was worrying the grass with his hand, pulling up blade after blade, his forehead bowed, his hair in stringy tufts, his lips pale.

'You should have been a philosopher, not a doctor,' he replied mildly.

Some gnats darted about in the air in erratic zigzags, never straying from their chosen space.

'I don't want to get you in any trouble. That much at least, for God's sake,' he went on softly.

'But if Vincenzo, on the other hand—' the girl ventured.

'Forget Vincenzo,' he cut in, his apparent impassivity overcome by some reserve of nervous energy. 'A shot behind the eye doesn't miss. Like in the mouth. Only in the mouth it shatters and for the others . . .'

I listened as I watched him, then her. For some reason they seemed very far away, and their words false and pointless. Nothing happened, ever: it's only one of those dreams in which he performs, dragging everything with him.

'Enough,' Sara pleaded.

'Enough,' he agreed, his head snapping from side to side. 'What should I ask you to do? Hang me? Throw me in the sea? So you two can be convicted? A cowardly bastard, but I won't go that far. We have no choice. Take me back there. Case closed. And let's stop arguing about it too. All these words, a useless waste of breath.'

'No!' Sara shot back.

'No, so then what?' He laughed drily, clenching his jaws. 'A fine solution. If all it took were a no.'

'I'm thirsty.' Sara sighed.

She stood up and took a couple of trailing steps around the tree, stretching her arms, disturbing the hovering gnats, which nevertheless quickly resumed frantically flitting about in their air space.

'A cigarette. Then we leave,' he said.

He silenced me with a gesture before I could attempt to respond.

'Wouldn't it be better if I went to have a look first? What would it take me? Maybe by this time . . . But then, no, never mind. We should stay here,' Sara started in again from behind the tree.

With a sudden impulse she went back to him, rested her temple against his shoulder, her eyes shut tight.

'Ciccio, you have to explain these girls to me.' He smiled weakly.

'It can't end like this. It can't. There must be a God,' Sara murmured.

'You hear how their mind works, Ciccio?' he said. Despite the humiliation of his crumpled shirt, the loosened collar and tie, there was something about his shoulders, the way he held his head, that still helped him go on.

'Don't talk about me as if I were like everyone else. As if I were those others. Please,' Sara protested without moving. She went on leaning her temple against that shoulder, like the muzzle of a pathetic dog hoping to be petted.

His ravaged face lost its composure under those assaults, barely holding it together.

'You've done way too much. You gave me time. I can never thank you enough. But that's enough now.' He tried again to soothe her.

'I didn't do anything. Ever.' Sara sighed. 'If only you had let me, then I would have.'

'Do you see anything special in yours truly, Ciccio? Something useful, I mean,' he went on.

'Everything about you is special,' I took pains to say.

He laughed nervously.

'Fool. Better yet: aspiring fool. And this bubblehead who instead of thinking about boys, thinks about me.'

'I would have found hundreds of them attractive, if you hadn't appeared,' Sara objected harshly, pulling away.

I searched for something to say to stop that kind of talk.

'Don't you want me to call Turin? Or your cousin in Rome?' I managed.

He feigned a shudder of revulsion. Wearily he replied, 'Your shift is over.'

'Please,' Sara began murmuring in that dogged monotone. 'A minute ago . . . Things were different. You too were different. You were asleep. I felt so happy. The first time in my life. It's not my imagination. Then you wake up and everything changes again. Who on earth can keep up with you? It can't end like this, it's not possible. Before—'

'There never was any before. Never. Get those foolish notions out of your head,' he snapped.

The creases on his forehead had become a deep mesh.

'What kind of a man are you! You don't even ask for help, don't even say you're sorry . . .' Sara cried.

I was already on my feet, ready to leave, when a brusque order was promptly fired up at me.

'Get her out of here. Take her into the house. Leave me in peace for a couple of minutes.'

Sara ran, then turned around to study him; uncertain, she went to take shelter against the wall.

I no longer had the faintest idea but I clearly felt the prick of satisfaction their argument had produced. In three hours we were back to being separate and apart like before, raking up anxieties and concerns.

I saw him take a long swig from the bottle and finally feel the trunk of the tree, the grass around him, that head of his like a nervous pendulum.

I climbed up into the trees, the parched ground crunching. When I reached the top of that bastion I saw other houses scattered about, modest roofs and terraces, gardens too, and in the distance a bumpy stretch of patched asphalt, shining in the sun. A truck passed by on it, then the colourful sweaters of three cyclists appeared in a row. They struggled up the incline, their backs curved and spotted like beetles.

Almost noon by my watch. I went back to the meagre shade along the wall, sat down next to Sara; both of us were intent on the tree in front, the gestures manoeuvring the bottle.

'Let them come. Let them all come. Bastards and swine. Let it be over,' I heard her say.

She accepted a cigarette and we smoked in silence for several long minutes, the dusty tips of our shoes lined up in front of us; the heat seemed to send vague shimmers through the air, lightning-fast flashes of light.

'Do you believe in love?' she asked suddenly, turning away, a roughness in her throat.

I tensed. 'I don't know. You?'

'In mine. Only in mine. In mine, I do. All the rest, the world and this life, is nothing. You tell me what really exists. Name me one thing, one single thing that's decent.'

'Sara,' I protested.

'Let it all go to hell,' she grumbled.

'We're sitting here talking about life, love, he's there drinking, and meanwhile the lieutenant . . .' But my own voice sounded false even though the image of Vincenzo swayed before me for a moment, light and airy, inflated like a colourful balloon figure.

'Would you stop talking about the lieutenant! Who is he to you? Your brother? You didn't even know him the day before yesterday,' she retorted hoarsely. 'All about whether one or two shots were fired. That's all you're interested in.'

'That's not true. You're the one who lacks sympathy. For you he's the only one who counts, no matter what he does or doesn't do . . .'

'Exactly. That's how it is.'

'Let's hope he doesn't get drunk again. Great idea, the bottle.' I pointed to the tree.

'He'll get drunk. What else can he do?' she replied slowly. 'Or maybe not even. That small amount of whisky can't be enough.'

'Do you really think he wanted to die?'

'Before. Not now. Not any more,' she said reluctantly. 'Now he's actually a different person. Still the same, yet different. So many flies here. And I'm so thirsty. Has the water come back maybe?'

Beyond the trees, a dog barked in the distance.

'Who knows what the newspapers are saying. Have you thought about that?'

'That's just what I want to think about, the newspapers, of course.' She scoffed at me, disheartened.

'And yet it's not every day that a blind man—'

'Don't say blind. Don't call him disabled. Don't *ever* let me hear you.' She recovered the spirit to stop me.

'You close your eyes and hope that things will change. That's what you do. Nice trick.'

She denied it, shaking her head.

'You'll never understand. Not if you live to be a hundred. Not even if they drilled it into your head,' she replied quietly. 'It's not your fault. It's no one's fault.'

The tips of her shoes kept playfully moving apart and back together again. She stubbed out her cigarette in the dirt, twisting her fingers.

'Then too even if you understood, all of you, a lot I care,' she added. Understanding – from you, from all of you – is just the treasure I need, what one dreams of at night.'

'Okay. I won't understand. You'll understand everything. Only you two will know it all. You and that other one. But now drop it. We'd better go back. What are we doing here? What are you still hoping for?' I said impatiently.

'Hope, despair, what's it to you?' she retorted bitterly. 'Do you think there's something you can teach me? There's nothing I can learn from you, not a thing, ever.'

'Good for you.' I turned to laugh at her. 'Now I've made up my mind, so long and amen. I should have done it sooner. And you two who are so clever: fend for yourselves.'

She had no strength left to react. The anger that barely rose to her face vanished in a slight grimace. The tips of her shoes nervously sped up the pace of their tapping.

'All the better. Right. Whether you stay or go, does anything change?' she replied in a faint voice. 'If you at least manage to get away, then go. I won't think badly of you, I swear.'

'Sara, but why . . .' A groan escaped me.

She lowered her eyes, biting her lips not to cry.

I took her hand; I felt those cold, stiff fingers of hers between my own.

She allowed it in silence.

I moved my hand to caress her, my fingertips lightly grazing her cheek, the top of her neck. Her skin was smooth and barely warm. She moved away slowly, stopping me.

'I can run down for something cool. An orange drink – want me to? I'll gladly go.'

She shrugged.

'I may certainly not be a great beauty. Definitely not,' she murmured. 'But I'm young. Someone might find me appealing. What did I ever ask of him? To marry me? No. Not at all. To be together, that's all. Marriage and children and respectability and all those other syrupy things, I never thought about them, not me.'

My hands felt awkward, I stuck them in my pocket, slumped against the wall.

'How can a man say no, always no?' she added.

'He's not a man. He's not like the others,' I replied, resigned.

'With just one word, he could have me. Just one.'

She said it without embarrassment, her chin lowered.

'What do you think? My fault because I don't know what's what? You heard him: "bubblehead", that's what he thinks of me. Is he right? I don't know what to think any more. My head is pounding . . .'

'He's afraid,' was all I could say. 'Maybe he's even thought about it, but he's ashamed and is afraid of taking advantage.

And now, at this point, he's zero. Zero plus zero, after every-thing that's happened, and he knows it.'

'Every other word for you is "now". Always this "now" that comes out of your mouth,' she said slowly, her arms wrapped around her knees, her pale face as transparent as fine muslin. 'Instead, nothing can change for me, for him. Not even if the wrath of God were to descend. Nothing will change. I say "never". Not your "now".'

I tried to change the subject: 'We should take the bottle away from him. Just look at him.'

'I'm looking, I'm looking; what is there to see?' She continued in the same half-hearted murmur. 'Let him do what he wants. Drink, shout. Anything, as long as he feels alive.'

'You're not being rational any more. You don't want to think rationally.'

'Does being rational do any good?' She laughed. 'Tell me: does one survive by being rational? Take a look around.'

'You should look around. You're not being fair.'

She agreed sadly. 'I'm not fair. Why should I be? What does your fairness have to do with me?'

'Sara . . .'

'Don't beat yourself up.'

Neither of us had raised our voice. The words came out in a whisper and quickly subsided, anxious and concerned.

'Sara, you can't go on this way. You're intelligent, and . . .'

'I don't want to hear about it. Not about fairness or intelligence or a thousand other things,' she murmured.

I snapped: 'Fine, then drop it. I'm going down. To make a call. To your house. You don't believe me? Wait and see. It's insane to stay here for hours having these conversations. You're out of your head.'

She rolled her shoulders, threw her head back as if to let out some kind of laugh.

'An obvious discovery. Good for you,' she replied from the depths of the spell that held her, though with a certain irony, and a resignation that was undoubtedly not due to exhaustion, or awareness of danger, a resignation that was more intimate, that went further back. 'It's obvious that I've lost my mind. I had one, and it's for him alone. You're kind though, you're also a man: what do you think? He can't keep saying no to me until judgment day. Can he? He'll have to understand, he'll have to take pity. He's bound to by his nature, as a human being. Answer me. Because if not, I have a hundred years of this agony waiting for me.'

I4

In the fluid air which expanded and contracted before my eyes in braided streaks and filaments, a dark spot began to float, running and sliding as though on a slope until it took on a solid form: the face and hair of the soldier Miccichè.

He moved a few cautious inches behind the blinding outline of the car, parked in the sun among the weeds. He peered around, eagerly taking in the house and clearing, the pale spot that was him against the tree, me in the garden.

He winked to get my attention.

As I walked towards him he backed away, a thousand hand signals urging caution, silence.

I caught up with him around the curve of the track; his gaze was veiled with suspicion.

'And the girl?' he whispered.

'Sara? Inside. In the house. There's almost no water. She's trying to collect some.'

Dully I looked at that faded uniform of his, the shirtsleeves rolled up above his elbows, the pockets sagging.

'Have you been here all along? What a situation. And nothing to eat besides.' He smiled. 'But all in all you're okay. All of you.'

He had big teeth blackened by smoking.

We faced each other in full sunlight, squinting in the brightness, his face tilted to one side and dry as a lizard. All my doubts were suddenly put to rest in the unexpected calm expressed by his presence.

'A cigarette. Or are you out?' he asked placidly, amused. I breathed again.

Now he'll tell me all about it, he'll explain the whole thing, everything will be restored to order, whatever that may be, let's hope, if only we get out of this limbo. Instead he was slow to utter the first word.

He sat down at the edge of the path after examining the dusty grass very carefully, his still unlit cigarette in his mouth, a vague, shrewd smile.

'Her mother—' He made up his mind at last with a self-important smile. '. . . the screams. The despair. A mother, you know. Try and imagine.'

Slowly, in detail and with a few studied pauses, he got on with the story.

Sara's mother herself had thought of the house while Ines, Michelina, Candida, in a frenzy, speculated about trains, the highway, even a ship. Candida had actually been slapped for too much talking and agitation. Urged by the woman, Miccichè had then taken off on his motor scooter, wasting time among tracks that were all the same. The lieutenant wasn't dead, not at all; the bullet must have been deflected by a bone. He was in the hospital now, he'd had two transfusions already and was not in any further danger.

'I'd be willing to swear to it: in a few days he'll be home again. With that constitution of his, healthy as a horse. He himself could still give blood. Did he shoot himself? Was he shot? Or maybe nothing more than a mistake? Only God

Almighty knows. Because he, first at home and later at the hospital, didn't utter a single word. And I don't think he ever will.'

A tingling sensation scampered along the walls of my stomach, like a laugh incapable of exploding.

No one in the entire building had heard the shot, or was it shots? Sara's mother had been the first to make the discovery, though accidentally, spurred by her womanly concern for those men, friends and customers, who had been left alone in the house without even a housekeeper. Fortunately she found the door open. A pharmacist on night-duty provided first aid, to stop the bleeding. A good friend. That's how the morning had begun, all a distraught hustle and bustle . . .

'I arrived later, fortunately in uniform, because of some business at the barracks. A uniform protects you. You did well to put yours back on too . . .'

Certainly at the police precinct they were regretful about the disappearance of the captain from Turin. Perhaps that captain, though he too was blind, would have been able to shed some light on certain things: a fit of madness on the part of his friend, or any other motives that might have come up at the family party. But actually no one doubted that it was madness; among the severely disabled it is precisely the well-to-do, who have no issues of immediate survival, who suffer the most and sometimes lose heart to the point of harming themselves and others . . .

'Though there are exceptions. For example, a man in my neighbourhood, also blind but sharp as a tack, you should see him eat, drink, play checkers . . .'

In any case the Commissioner himself – swearing angrily

as he sent away two news-hungry journalists – had very compassionately interpreted the guest's disappearance as natural, surely motivated by emotion, despair, being powerless to help . . .

'A very kind person, this Commissioner. But when you talk to him, watch your step. Because he always yeses you, but you have to repeat things to him a thousand times. For all his sensitivity, he's more adamant than a tank.'

I too had surely been a victim of that same despair. Poor dim-witted soldier, far from home. Who knows where I might be now with my captain clinging to my arm? They assumed we were missing but still in the city; with the help of God we would recover our senses, we would go back. Or some agent would recognize us, a matter of hours . . .

'They left a policeman at the house, not a detective, only a uniformed officer. Another thing: who wiped down the gun? Do you want to know? The caretaker. A poor old woman, not even the Commissioner had the heart to scold her. Here too, God showed His hand, believe it or not.'

In fact there had never been any talk of wrongdoing, there was no suspect, no charges, only the shadow of fate, the unfair, malevolent caprice of an existence that carries everyone along, affords no peace to any creature on this earth . . .

'Do you get my drift? When it comes to well-bred gentlemen, even adversity puts on white gloves. That's how it is.' He peered at me from hooded eyelids.

'What about Sara?' I asked.

He spread his arms in resignation before responding.

'Little or nothing was said. Her mother quickly explained that the young woman was in bed, she didn't feel well, too many iced drinks. Of course tomorrow she'll have to appear.

The Commissioner, that fine gentleman, is just like I described, he may call you "sir", but he questions you, he telephones. And who knows what he may still be thinking? She has to show up, the young lady. Tomorrow. Maybe even better tonight.'

I saw an electric charge go through the air. And that crawling sensation in my stomach tingled no end.

'That's how it is,' the soldier repeated looking up at me. 'You're laughing? Lucky you, then.'

But I wasn't able to. My throat was parched, stifled.

'Plain crazy,' he said between sighs, his eyes downcast again. 'But the whole world is that way. You just have to be forewarned.'

'Yeah,' I said. 'Right.'

My eyes held a vision, ridiculous but real: a kind of toy track, with lots of tiny cars racing along; swiftly they devour the space ahead of them, mindlessly perfect. And we were just like them. Something had held us in a vacuum, something else now set us back in motion.

'But you, didn't your leave expire?' he was really worried. 'Don't take a chance and leave that way. Have them issue you something in writing. From the precinct, from your captain if he's still aware of what's going on. Or even from the Commissioner. Listen to me. Do you want to pay for other people's messes?'

'No, no.'

He raised his sharp face again.

'And the young lady? I mean, did anything happen?'

'What?' I said, realizing too late.

He was already raising his hands in surrender.

'Why are you looking at me that way?' he shot back,

satisfied. 'I was just asking. What harm would there be? In these situations, with all the anxiety, the darkness, the confusion. A man is still a man. Things happen. But then she only has eyes for that other one, the crazy one, right? I forgot.'

'She's a good girl,' I reproached him foolishly.

'Of course. Who would deny it?' he agreed, surprised. 'But even good girls can be fun like the others. Maybe even more so.'

I glanced towards the curve of the path, certain I would see Sara. Though on the other hand she might have fallen asleep or joined him under the tree again.

'You: were you there?' Miccichè asked in his most distracted tone.

'We heard. From the courtyard.'

'Didn't see? Anything?'

'Only heard. Then—'

He quickly gestured for me to stop.

'I don't want to know,' he said bluntly. 'The less I know the better it is. Still, you'll have to tell the Commissioner something. And always the same thing, like a broken record. Think about it ahead of time. You can say you were sleeping. Or that you had too much to drink. No, wait: not drunk. For those people being drunk is always an aggravating circumstance.'

I pointed behind him.

'I'll have to talk with him about it.'

He shook his head in disgust.

'Bravo. You really found your man. First he drowns you, then he asks you if you're all right; first he grinds you into the dirt, then he asks you if you liked it, if you're okay.'

'You don't know him.'

'And I don't want to know him. Still, he's a gentleman and you'll get to hell before him.' He laughed, showing his long teeth.

I laughed too. 'Are you a communist?'

He pointed a finger at me. 'There are situations where I can talk like a communist. But I don't get worked up over politics. I have enough troubles of my own. And you, what are you?'

'Nothing,' I said, 'I don't believe in those things. Never have.'

He nodded gravely. 'You're right,' he said, 'everyone has to solve his own problems. A small fish swims fast, too many small fish together attract nets.'

'Still, I envy them, those others. United, they keep each other company. At least it seems that way.'

'*Seems*. Exactly. It's all show.' He rubbed his nose vigorously up and down. 'Mules get along well together, thoroughbred horses don't. Though this is a world that is more and more for mules. All shouting the same things. Do you get me? Because I'm glad to be your friend. A friend from another place is always an advantage in life.'

'A records clerk, you told me the other day. What preparation have you had? Or are you still studying?'

He pulled a long face, glum. 'I've already finished my schooling. But they were worthless studies. A records clerk, true, that too, but in the near future. I have an uncle on my mother's side in the public records department, at the town hall. He's holding a post for me, for when I finish military duty. Some fun, huh? But first this famous job and then we'll see. But why are we still here talking? It's hot, the sun is blazing, we haven't eaten and you have the Commissioner to think about. Slippery as an eel, that's how you have to be. And the captain? Up at the house?'

'No. Back there. He's probably drinking.'

'You fell for it,' he rebuked me sadly. 'You took him seriously. Me, as soon as I saw him, I said to myself: a Punchinello. A skinny, dried-up buffoon who swallowed his stick to stand up straight and—'

He broke off, pointed a thumb towards the path. I saw Sara silhouetted against the light. She was coming towards us, managing not to quicken her step. She seemed more refreshed, her eyes serene; maybe she had slept in the last half hour. Without a word she held out her hand to Miccichè, who had stood up again.

My brief flicker of happiness was quickly reduced to cinders in the depths of my heart.

'Let him explain it to you. He knows everything,' I said moving away. 'I'm going back to him. Still there?'

'The lieutenant won't talk. He'll never talk. Not even if they skinned him alive. That's the truth. That's the important thing you have to know,' Miccichè mumbled again, looking at nothing and no one. 'And given that, go ahead and fabricate your own scenario.'

'So he isn't dead and I seem to be alive,' he pronounced as soon as I finished telling him.

He tried to smile, his lined face belying his actual age. He shrank back against the tree in the last remaining arc of shade, the bottle almost empty.

'Poor Vincenzino. The failure. The absurdity . . .' he went on, the fingernails of his right hand picking at the stubble on his cheek, his chin.

In the distance, the regular pounding of a hammer.

He then tried to move his left arm. The rigid glove dangled.

'I'm coming unhinged.'

And he laughed, a single burst like a sob.

'I feel filthy,' he began complaining again. 'How stupid, right? And yet if I were washed and my clothes pressed everything would seem different. Ah, that bar of ours in Rome. Remember? A match, Ciccio. Even the lighter doesn't work any more. So much for our fine self-sufficiency.'

I went all around the tip of the cigarette, lighting it carefully.

'The fog,' he continued softly, 'do you remember our fog? In Turin? And its scent, the finest in the world. The one in November is the best. I'm not drunk, Ciccio, don't worry. But you, doesn't this dry air bother you?'

I pictured my city, the viewer speckled like the film of an old movie, black and white, in grainy filaments, light drizzles. And I felt a great, slow desire to be reabsorbed in it, to wander about that screen without my true face any more.

An insect with transparent purplish wings was climbing along his jacket. I flicked it away with my fingernail.

'Know what I am? The eleven of spades. My father was right. With each failure, or when money disappeared from the drawer of the pharmacy, he took it out on my mother: you drew the eleven of spades; now we have to put up with it.'

He smiled, blowing smoke.

'But there is no eleven of spades,' I objected.

'Exactly. A card that isn't in the deck. Not good for playing any game,' he approved, the cigarette following the movement of his lips, his neck rigid in an effort of will.

Again he said, 'Poor Vincenzino, if you had come to my house maybe now . . .'

I don't want to listen to you any more, I thought.

I had an ache between the back of my neck and my shoulder, fatigue rankling in my body. There seemed to be no remedy.

'What do you plan to do, sir?'

'Sir. Lord. Heavenly Father. Great God in heaven, if only I were a little swallow,' he mocked, but very weakly.

Then: 'Don't worry, my friend. Today, tonight, you're leaving. And you won't have any trouble. My word. If you still trust it.'

'I wasn't talking about me.'

'Are you hungry?'

'Yes,' I replied.

'Good, me too. Incredible. I'm stinking filthy, a lost cause, if I fire a shot I miss that too, I land whoever may be around in trouble, yet I'm hungry. Simple, right?'

He laughed again, sprinkling cigarette ash on himself.

'What do I plan to do, you ask? Surrender. And trust in the generosity of the enemy.'

'Who is?'

'Who is: you'll see. Or actually, no. You won't see a damn thing.' He slumped back, bowing his head.

Sara was returning. Miccichè was already standing mistrustfully beside the car; when I motioned him to come over, he replied no with his head, his hand. He sat down next to a wheel without looking at us.

'Fausto, I'm here. Have you heard? What if it's a trap?' the girl said.

'Sara, Sara, why aren't you like the other girls?' He still tried to smile at her.

She shuffled her feet sombrely in the grass, her eyes downcast.

'I'll end up that way. Thanks to this, thanks to that, I too will end up like all the others. Some good it will do me, for my future,' she responded.

'You talk like you're already widowed!' He tried to laugh, but the effort was so pathetic that Sara just looked at him, without the heart to answer him back.

'I could put the suitcase in the car,' I said.

'Hold it. First a swig. Let's not abandon our routines so quickly,' he said, retrieving the bottle. 'And don't slink off all the time, you.'

Sara's hostile gaze was on me.

'Fausto, it's a trap. I can feel it,' she started in again.

'Okay, okay. I get it. All the better,' he said, exasperated.

Miccichè was now studying us, his fingers gesturing questioningly, trying to hurry me up.

'We have to go,' he decided.

'Where should I take you?' the girl asked quietly.

He replied curtly, 'The first carabiniere.'

'Fausto . . .'

'So be it. Not a word.'

Sara nodded, her hands upside-down in her lap, her ashen face expressionless.

'I just meant, would you like to take a bath, freshen up a little?' she said softly. 'Shall I take you to my house? It would only take a minute, what's one minute . . .'

'And your mother?' he said, surprised.

'I don't care. About anyone. Just let them try to stop me,' she retorted harshly. 'And keep in mind: I'm going with you, I'm taking you there. And if I have to keep quiet, I'll keep quiet. But I'm staying with you till the end.'

'What does that mean?'

'That I'm staying with you until the others kick me out, even forcibly. Not you.'

'I won't send you away again. Not me,' he replied weakly. And turned his head.

I saw a shudder pass between Sara's shoulders.

'Swear,' she whispered. Her hand which had already reached out shrank back, frightened, clasping the other hand.

'Yes, yes. I swear. You heard me. But that's enough now,' he murmured, overcome.

15

I can't help remembering.

It all happened as if seen through inverted binoculars: me perpetually, breathlessly in pursuit of faces, glimpses, shadows, fragments of images quickly lost, which only the mysterious powers of a dream could produce.

It all ended the exact same way.

Except it wasn't a dream.

Today I remember Sara's actions, sober, thought out. Unhurriedly, she cleaned him up with a wet handkerchief, from his temples to the corners of his mouth, his right hand one fingernail at a time. She straightened his collar, his tie.

He was docile, unaware.

And Miccichè, who kept saying, 'Will they hurry up? Where the hell do they think they're going? To the opera?'

Then they set out in the car, while I sat on the back seat of the motor scooter, clinging to Miccichè.

I can no longer describe the exhaustion I felt then. The body is blessed because it forgets. But I recall all too well my impervious mind, its desire to rush headlong into a whirlwind and run and run.

Passing them, driving side by side, having them pass us in

turn, I never saw them exchange a word, she alert at the wheel, he reclining.

The road was all curves, the air fiery, stinging between my shirt and skin.

Naples swallowed us up almost immediately.

Our goodbyes at the end were very brief.

'So long, Ciccio,' he fired at me with feigned energy. 'Here. Forget all this.'

I kept my papers, but handed the money to Sara, who slipped it into her belt.

'Catch your train. Go. Don't worry,' he added, 'I'll protect you. When it's time, it's time. I'm turning myself in: even the combat manuals say so. And keep in mind, I'll tell the truth. If you're forced to, tell yours as well.'

His was no longer a face but a withered leaf.

'Say goodbye to our friend,' he suggested to Sara.

We were on a street corner. It seemed to me that the sliver of sea back there was not far from the lieutenant's house.

Sara did not speak. She shook my hand. After a moment they disappeared arm-in-arm.

I still remember Miccichè, who was also silent.

He drove through narrow streets and alleys before finding a pizzeria that appealed to him. He insisted on paying with the few lire he had, no question about it. A train at 3.03 p.m., we managed to find out.

'Can I write to you? Will you give me your address?' I can still hear his voice. 'What did you leave at the lieutenant's house? Razor, clothes? I'll take care of it. You go, you have to leave. I'll see to it, I'll send them. Trust me.'

He accompanied me to the station, following me to the ticket office, then the bathroom. I bought him a coffee at the bar. Not another word amid all that noise. His eyes had grown sad, like when a party's over.

'Too bad. I'm really sorry. But you can't stay here. For now that's the way it is,' he said simply.

The waiters pushed and shoved behind the counter in their frantic haste to serve and clear away.

Despite the coffee, my mouth felt gritty.

And if at the time I felt like a traitor, a louse, even today I can't forgive myself for that getaway – so violently, absurdly hasty.

I could still see him and Sara in my mind's eye, their last steps before they turned the corner, their stride spirited, not at all resigned.

'I'll write to you. I'll send your stuff. Don't give it another thought,' Miccichè added, leaning on the counter.

The truth is, we didn't know what to say to one another.

Suddenly a lengthy procession of young people with placards and banners marched across the square in front of the station. Through the windows we saw them advance like a large speckled fish, its head swollen and throbbing, its stunted tail trailing along here and there.

It was Miccichè who said, 'Look at them. Crazies. Can't you just see signorina Sara leading them all? I can. She's the one who made a mistake.'

The banners and signs were soon dissolved by the light, swaying rhythmically as they disappeared.

The train was empty, an inferno. Miccichè went up and down the aisle opening one window after another.

'Will you be able to get some sleep in there?' he added before getting off, appraising the fake leather seats suspiciously. 'A good nap is all the medicine you need.'

I watched him grow smaller at the end of the tracks.

Razor and clothes arrived at the barracks in about a week, after I had already given my deposition to an official from the carabinieri who had come to question me.

It was boring and simple.

Nothing ever appeared in the newspapers, and I truly believe that there will be no trial. Almost two months have passed. These nights Turin smiles, gives off the sweet fragrance of petals, while I still have not been able to find answers to my questions.

Was the captain sincere when he surrendered to Sara?

Or was he fooling her to make things go more smoothly?

And the lieutenant: has he talked?

I could call Fausto G.'s home; someone would answer, I'd be able to gather some news.

But a game like this isn't won by moving and eliminating a weak piece here and there on the chessboard.

Only now do I understand that if a young woman like Sara won, I too should stop reproaching myself. On the contrary, I acquired things in which I can hope, for tomorrow, for myself.

It takes love to attract and nurture love. With her fierce intelligence, Sara taught me this, albeit unconsciously. And today, whether I am an ant or a grasshopper, a hare or a dog, whether the world is a biblical scourge or a miserable day-by-day trap doesn't matter, as long as Sara's example can give me courage, a courage of my own, for myself, for the niche I have to carve out and inspire in life.

There's him on the other hand, a dark shadow . . .

Perhaps it wasn't only his misfortune, perhaps it wasn't simply his despair that made him want to die. Maybe he saw death as a decisive rendezvous with himself, a final settling of accounts.

Because there is also a kind of man who can only be explained by dying.

But if instead he's close by or somewhere else and, despite the dark prison that has confined him for years, continues flicking his cigarette lighter, thrashing the air with his bamboo cane, mocking and insulting and drinking – with Sara at his side – then the most difficult condition of life is nevertheless living. For him and for me. For all of us who are able to acknowledge, accept and nurture it.

And the blank space that follows is not yet death.

PENGUIN MODERN CLASSICS

THE LAST PICTURE SHOW
LARRY MCMURTRY

With a new Introduction by Mary Carr

Sam the Lion runs the pool-hall, the picture house and the all-night café. Coach Popper whips his boys with towels and once took a shot at one when he disturbed his hunting. Billy wouldn't know better than to sweep his broom all the way to the town limits if no one stopped him. And teenage friends Sonny and Duane have nothing better to do than drift towards the adult world, with its temptations of sex and confusions of love.

The basis for a classic film, *The Last Picture Show* is both extremely funny and deeply profound – a timeless story of coming of age in small town Texas.

'An alchemist who converts the basest materials into gold'
The New York Times Book Review

'There aren't many writers around who are as much fun as Larry McMurtry'
Boston Globe

PENGUIN MODERN CLASSICS

THE ROAD TO SAN GIOVANNI
ITALO CALVINO

'Brimming with Calvino's beautifully crafted prose, dry humour and continual questioning of his own writing and memory' *Observer*

The Road to San Giovanni contains five autobiographical essays – fascinating expeditions through the memories of one of the greatest writers of the twentieth century. In these elegant meditations Calvino delves into his past, remembering awkward childhood walks with his father, a lifelong obsession with the cinema and fighting in the Italian Resistance against the Fascists. He also muses on the social contract, language and sensations associated with emptying the kitchen rubbish and the shape he would, if asked, consider the world. These reflections on the nature of memory itself are engaging, witty and lit through with Calvino's alchemical brilliance.

'Urbane and always elegant ... shows us what a master we have lost in Italo Calvino' *Literary Review*